FAIR TRADE

My Mira, Part Three

DUSTIN STEVENS

*Catch on fire and people will
come for miles to see you burn.*
—John Wesley

Prologue

I SMELL it long before I see it. Whether it is a real scent or simply a figment of my mind, a psychosomatic response to the phone call a few minutes before, I have no idea.

What I know for sure is the smell of smoke is in the air. It seems to settle around me, thick as a fog. Every inhalation burns my nostrils, sliding into my lungs. My eyes are rimmed with moisture.

But again, I have no way of knowing if any of this is real. Or even a response to what I was just told.

As little as a few days ago, I might have considered this a good thing. I may have taken a step back, thought of everything we'd already been through, and decided to just let it go.

The instant I answered the phone though, such thoughts evaporated forever, as ethereal as morning fog, vaporized by the rising sun. And just like those bright early rays, what was left behind was so clear it was almost blinding. So obvious, I felt foolish for having not seen it sooner.

The red needle of the speedometer is pinned at a one-hundred-degree angle on the dash before me. Much faster than I have any business driving on the 805, I can't bring myself to slow down. I don't even acknowledge the other drivers around me with their honks and glares and middle fingers, my focus locked straight ahead.

A flick of my gaze to the dashboard shows it has been just three minutes since the call came in. So little by most any measurable standard, it now seems like an eternity, the full destructive power of one hundred and eighty seconds flashing through my mind.

One time after another, behind each blink of my eyes, conjured images come to mind. Snapshots of things I'd rather not even consider. Of deeds that cannot be undone.

Things that might very well snap the tenuous grasp on reality I've been clinging to for a solid week.

The front faceplate of my phone springs to life beside me, the light bright in the front cab of the car. Casting my gaze that direction, I recognize the name being displayed back at me, though I make no effort to answer.

Not now.

Right now, all I can focus on is my destination. On what might happen if I arrive to find everything I fear has actually come to pass.

Chapter One

FEW PLACES ARE EVER TRULY DOING business around the clock. Regardless if an establishment advertises itself as being available twenty-four hours or not, rare can it be said that the place is actually making transactions at anywhere near that pace.

Just drive past a 7-11 at three in the morning sometime. You'll see a vagrant asleep on the sidewalk outside, a poor immigrant working the graveyard shift to try and help make ends meet, and a whole lot of neon and halogen doing little more than wasting electricity.

Despite their radically different purposes, the same can be said for the Paradise Valley Hospital.

The place was picked for two simple reasons. It has an emergency department, and it is geographically the closest to the Chula Vista suburb of San Diego. If given the time or the inclination, there are a good handful of other places we definitely would have rather gone, but having the luxury of neither, this is where we ended up.

Six hours earlier, my brother-in-law Hiram and I had made the drive in from La Mesa – another suburb, this one on the eastern edge of the city sprawl. The trip was made with the simple goal in mind of having a conversation, of getting to sit down with the last unknown entry listed in my wife's date book before her senseless murder almost a week ago.

And, like damn near everything else that has transpired in the days since, the meeting turned out to be anything but what we expected.

My jaw aches slightly and a wicked headache is sitting just behind my left eye as I walk through the halls of Paradise Valley. Beside me is my diminutive mother-in-law, her steps short and choppy as we both make our way forward, headed toward the cafeteria.

I don't bother looking over at her as we march on, both of us locked in our own heads, trying to make sense of so damn much disparate information. Tonight was supposed to have finally started to crack open the tight package that everything seemed to be wrapped in, though at the moment, all I can conjure are more questions.

And a whole lot of anger.

The lights above have been dimmed to a third of their usual strength. With most of the patients asleep for the night and the staff reduced to a skeleton crew, there is no need for the extra expense, nobody around to use the illumination even if it was on. Long shadows fall across the tile floor as we walk, the low and even purr of a janitor running a buffer serving as background noise.

Coming up on a hallway crossing, I glance to the wall just long enough to check the signage. "To the left," I whisper, my mother-in-law responding with a light grunt.

Together, we make the turn and head over, finally coming to our destination a full five minutes after rising from the chairs outside Hiram's room. Neither of us have slept at all this evening, barely more than that in the preceding week, but it doesn't matter. We are both too locked in now to think of doing anything else.

Pushing straight through the double doors into the cafeteria, we find the space just as deserted as the rest of the hospital. Even fewer bulbs are burning along the ceiling, most of the light in the place coming from the residual glow of vending machines.

As we enter, the lone troupe of people inside turn our direction. Tucked away into the back corner, they represent one of the oddest assortments I imagine the room has ever housed, all with their mouths drawn into tight lines, staring intently back at us.

From what I can tell, nobody was saying a word before our arrival, everybody waiting for us, not bothering to go through the motions of getting acquainted.

Split into pairs, on the right are my friends Jeff Swinger and Emily Stapleton. Both people I first encountered in my time with the Navy, Jeff is a Chief Petty Officer, someone that I met in my first days of SEAL training and have been with ever since. Standing a few inches above six feet in height, he is heavily muscled, a poster child for the lucky bastards that seem to get ripped through little more than walking past a gym a couple times a week.

His dark hair is cut short with a few days of growth on his face. Since we're not the Army and don't care near as much about such things, I know in a few days it'll likely be back to a full beard, the look one that has come and gone too many times to count over the years. Dressed in gym shorts and a hoodie, the sleeves of it have been pushed up to mid-forearm, revealing bright tattoos along his left arm.

Standing, he has one foot on a chair. His forearms are crossed over the raised knee, his weight leaning forward, as if he is a sprinter about to spring forth out of the blocks.

Or as I know to be much closer to the truth, like a man that just needs to be pointed in the right direction before he explodes forward and starts kicking some serious ass.

Him and me both.

Sitting beside him is Emily Stapleton, an ensign that helps with logistics for our unit and a number of others working out of nearby Coronado. A year younger than me, she is just past thirty, with bright auburn hair pulled into a ponytail and a pale complexion. With a frame that suggests she too could be active duty, she is several inches taller than Mira had been, her shoulders square.

Dressed in yoga pants and a sweatshirt, I can see circles under her eyes. No doubt they are a result of me and this damnable situation, a fact I can't pretend doesn't press a pang deep into my core.

Never will she say a word about it, just as I would do the same in her position, but that doesn't stop the guilt from seeping in anyway.

Sitting opposite them are the two women that Hiram and I were intending to meet with hours before. Bearing little resemblance to each other beyond the dark hue of their skin, I know them to be Valerie Ogo and her grandmother Fran, though beyond that I admit to clutching at straws.

Who they are, why Mira was set to meet with them, why men immediately showed up and attacked us as soon as we arrived – all things I hope to begin answering in the coming moments.

"Is Hiram okay?" Stapleton asks, the words sounding abnormally loud in the quiet of the room.

I flick a glance to my mother-in-law, seeing she has no intention of saying anything just yet. Pulling my gaze back, I reply, "He will be. Acute anxiety attack from what happened."

"Which was what?" Swinger asks. The words aren't hostile, but there's a charge there I recognize instantly. Both from years of working with him, and from hearing the same sound in my own voice just hours before.

"Are you okay?" Stapleton adds no more than a split second later, seeing the effects of the unexpected shot I had taken earlier splayed across my cheek.

Opening my mouth to respond, I pull up short. There will be time to get into all of this, but right now I need to seize control of the narrative. What happened earlier shouldn't be the focus. Why it occurred has to be, at least initially.

Holding up a single finger, I force my focus away from my friends to the opposite side of the table. There, both women stare up at me, their eyes wide.

"Ladies, like I said earlier, my name is Kyle Clady. I am – *was* – Mira Clady's husband." Using the same finger, I point to my mother-in-law beside me. "And this is her mother, Angelique."

I pause a moment, waiting as they both look between us, before adding, "Now, again I ask, who the hell are you two?"

Chapter Two

WHEN HIRAM and I showed up earlier in the evening, my goal was to have a conversation. I'd seen the listing in my wife's work datebook, called and asked to sit down for a few minutes. The idea was that I would explain who I was, ask who they were, see if there was any reason to think they might be connected to her death.

I admit, it was a stretch. But days of digging through everything I had wasn't turning up a damn thing. No unexplained pieces of mail, no random messages jotted down anywhere.

My wife might not have been a saint, but she was one of the closest people I'd ever met to one. She didn't believe in grudges, had never had a mortal enemy. Not once had I ever heard her say a cross thing about a coworker or even the rude barista at the coffee shop she liked to go to.

The woman was the daughter of immigrants. She'd put herself through college on a racquetball scholarship, a game she'd picked up while spending time from an early age at the health club where her mother worked as a janitor.

Of the two of us, I was the one that had enemies. Maybe not by name or someone I might run into on the street, but the better part of a decade as a SEAL had put me into some of the worst sewers on the planet. And had caused me to do some things I would rather my mother never found out about.

If somebody was going to get shot down in a park, it should have been me. After it happened, that was my original thought even, that someone had been targeting me, had gotten nervous and missed at the worst possible moment.

A day later, I had tracked down the man that did it and taken him out into the desert, intent to make him pay for his mistake. And it was there, with his dying breaths, that I found out he hit exactly where he was aiming.

The why was the part I had spent every moment since trying to parse out.

Despite my original plan to sit down with the women and have a calm and reasonable discussion, what little patience I might have was obliterated by the scene a few hours prior. With my ear ringing and the dull throbbing in my cheek feeling like it might force my eyeball from its socket, I can already feel the agitation pulsating through me.

The best I can hope for is it to keep it somewhat intact throughout the course of this interaction.

The women both look scared as they stare up at me. Sitting closest is the older of the two. Wrapped in a fuzzy coat over sweatpants and a sweater, her hair is completely silver, her skin lined from years of sun exposure. Despite that, her gaze is clear, her energy strong.

Behind her sits a woman thirty or forty years her junior. Appearing in her late-twenties, she has long dark hair and dark eyes, her expression tinged with annoyance as she stares back at me.

"Like I told you back at home," she says, "my name is Valerie Ogo, and this is my grandmother Fran."

At the sound of her name, the old woman nods, though remains silent.

Returning the gesture, I motion with the top of my head toward the opposite side of the table. "And this Jeff and Emily. They are both in the Navy with me, were friends with my wife."

Valerie gives them no more than a quick glance before looking back my way. Her eyes narrowed slightly, she says, "That's twice now you've referred to Mira in the past tense. What the hell is going on here? And what was all that about earlier?"

A couple of times over the years, I've been in the unenviable position of having to interrogate someone. While we have specialists trained in such things, that only works when you have plenty of time and the right surroundings. Otherwise, you make do with what you have, extracting information on the fly and hoping for the best.

Again, enemies scattered throughout my past.

Never have I gone anywhere near what one might find going on in Guantanamo Bay, but I have had enough experience to at the very least know when someone is lying to me. And from what I can tell, Valerie Ogo is confused, she's pissed, she's worried, but she isn't lying.

Flicking my gaze to Swinger, I raise my eyebrows just slightly, an unspoken question passing between us. A quick shake of his head shows he is getting the same read, each of us turning our attention back to the far side of the table.

Like so many times in the preceding days, questions come flying to mind. Arriving from every angle, they pour in thick and furious, too many to be addressed in any kind of order.

Turning to the side, I grab the back of the nearest chair. Twisting it around, I slide it up behind Angelique. "Here, this could take a while."

Accepting with a silent nod, she lowers herself into it as I spread my feet, folding my arms across my chest. No amount of fatigue can offset the nervous energy passing through me, tiny bits of adrenaline from earlier in the night still lingering in my system.

"Last Thursday night, my wife and I were walking through Balboa Park," I say. "We'd had dinner with Jeff and Emily and another friend of ours and then went for a walk."

Pausing, I turn my head to the side, pulling in a deep breath through my nose. With it comes the three millionth viewing of the incident in my mind, the man's face still so clear, his words ringing in my mind.

"Where a man shot and killed her. Point blank, in cold blood."

I decide to leave out the parts about us later tracking the man down and ending his life in a most severe and painful way. Such details aren't at all relevant to what I need right now.

"Oh my God," Valerie says, the previous angst disappearing from her face. Her features fall flat as she raises a hand to her chest, her mouth sagging slightly. "I'm so sorry."

Brushing past her condolences, I continue, "And as he was fleeing, he made a statement to the effect of, it was intentional."

To either side of me, Angelique, Swinger, and Stapleton all remain silent. All three know the way things really played out. The latter two were there and had an active role in it. But nobody says a word to correct me, their own reasoning likely matching my own.

There are more important things at hand than burdening these women with the truth.

"Intentional?" Valerie asks. Her face screws up slightly, some of the confusion from earlier returning to her features. "Mira?"

"So you knew her well?" I ask, seizing on her use of my wife's first name.

For a moment, there is no response. Valerie simply sits and tries to digest the information, her gaze drifting to the empty table between them as she chews on things. Eventually, she looks up, the skin crinkled around her eyes. "I...I just never would have..."

So badly I want to reach out and grab her by the shoulders. To tell her to look at me, to focus on what I'm saying, to answer the questions I'm throwing her way.

Just as surely, I know I can't. The news I just shared is a bombshell. The rest of us around the table have spent the better part of a week trying to come to grips with it. This woman has had a few seconds.

"How well did you know her?" I repeat.

Shifting her eyes up to look at me, Valerie shakes her head. "Not well. I'd only met once before, and that was an arranged thing. Nana had never met her."

"What do you mean, *an arranged thing*?" Angelique asks, the sound of her voice pulling the attention of both women her way.

Fran remains silent. Behind her, Valerie casts a glance around the table, checking each of us in turn.

"Please don't find my grandmother rude. She isn't conversing because she doesn't understand a word of what's going on."

I can see a crease form between Stapleton's eyes at the comment, the words seemingly coming from far afield.

"Chuukese," I say, recalling my initial encounter with the woman, standing on her front porch. "I recognized it earlier."

Valerie's eyebrows go up slightly. "You've been to Micronesia?"

Shaking my head slightly, I motion with my chin toward Swinger. "Jeff and I were stationed in Guam for a while. There's a large Chuuk population there."

The crease fades from Stapleton's brow as she gazes back at Valerie. Behind her, Swinger nods slightly in understanding.

"Oh," Valerie replies, "so then you're familiar with the term COFA."

Before I have a chance to respond, Angelique inserts herself into the conversation. "I'm sorry, I don't mean to be rude this time, but I'm still not sure what any of this has to do with my question. What did you mean, *an arranged meeting*?"

Already, I have some idea of where Valerie is going with all this, but I can understand my mother-in-law's unease. The question she posed was fairly simple, though already I can tell the response is going to be cloaked in layers.

Each one seeming to bring a sense of dread to my core.

"I was introduced to your daughter by a doctor," Valerie says. "A man named Brendan Hoke that works out of a local clinic in National City."

Shifting her focus back up to me, Valerie says, "Dr. Hoke is known to kind of be the first stop for COFA migrants coming into the city. People like my Nana here. He gives them a onceover, and if everything is okay, he sends them on their way.

"If not, he puts them in touch with people that might be able to help."

The answer is circuitous, but fits pretty close with what I was expecting the moment she mentioned COFA.

"People like my Mira," I whisper.

"Exactly," Valerie says, nodding slightly. "We were supposed to have all sat down again together last Friday, but..."

She doesn't finish the sentence. She doesn't need to.

Chapter Three

REACHING OUT, Ringer presses the button on the side of his cellphone, illuminating the front screen. Raising his chin just slightly, he peers down his nose at the digital readout across the top of it, white numbers against a plain black background.

"Four minutes after four," he says, his voice drawing the stares of the few men remaining around the table where he sits.

The place is known as The Wolf Den, a simple bar built on the outskirts of El Cajon, the town itself a jumping off point from the sprawl of San Diego into the desert that comprises the bottom half of the state. Constructed more than two decades before with a very specific clientele in mind, the place serves as the very definition of the phrase *no frills*.

Made entirely from wood and nails, small creases are visible between the floorboards, years of drying under the southern sun having done its worst. Along one wall, a bar runs the length of the room, waist-high, the front edge rubbed smooth from years of sweaty forearms leaning against it.

Behind it is the same barkeep that has been present since the place opened, the migration of his hair from black to silver the only sign that any time has passed.

Despite the hour, he is still posted behind the bar. In his hand is a dog-eared Louis L'Amour paperback, a pair of spectacles balanced on the end of his nose. Every so often, he glances to the corner, making sure his guests are good, before going back to reading.

Most nights, the place would have closed hours before. It being the middle of the week, the men would have left sometime around midnight, retreating back to their homes in anticipation of whatever they had going the next day.

For some, that is work. For others, a host of different possibilities as varied as the men that congregate there, the largest similarity – in some cases the *only* similarity – the men have being the leather vests they wear and the motorcycles they ride.

Events of the last week have changed that, though. It has taken what should have been a standard evening and turned the volume up exponentially.

Which is why Ringer, the leader of the Wolves, and his three deputies are still seated in the corner. And the barkeep is still behind the bar.

Just as they all will continue to be for as long as it takes to see things through.

"Any word from our guys yet?" Ringer asks.

Raising his gaze, he glances around the table, opening the floor for discussion.

To his left sits Byrdie, a man that many assumed would ascend to the top when it came open a few years prior. A bit older than Ringer, he is the smallest of the four men present, his entire being carved from cord and tendon. Wearing only a ribbed tank top beneath his vest, his bare arms gleam under the overhead light, every ridge visible beneath the skin.

The hair on either side of his head is shaved down to the scalp, the top and back left long, hanging down his back.

Those things have all been there for years. The newest addition is the fact that the entire left side of his face looks like it has been hit by a city bus. Misshapen and puffy, bruising has already set in, his cheek appearing to have been fractured, an open wound sprouting from the corner of his mouth.

A result of the encounter earlier evening that is a part of what has the men so agitated, he sits in silence, unable to say a word.

Directly across from him is the other half of the team that had been sent out, a man different from Byrdie in every way. Known as Gamer inside the organization, he weighs the better part of three hundred pounds, all of it the sort of dense flesh that could be either muscle or fat.

His head shaved bald, heavy droplets of sweat shine from his scalp, no matter the hour or the cool air floating in through the front swinging doors.

Between them is the third deputy for the organization. Known as Snapper, a mouthful of yellowed teeth juts out from between his lips, altering his appearance and his voice in equal parts.

"The guys are in position," Snapper says.

Flicking his glance down to the darkened screen of his phone, Ringer says, "It's after four. Nothing?"

Eighteen hours earlier, Ringer had been approached by a woman that had done business with Mike Lincoln – Linc – a fully vested member of the Wolves. Known to pay the bills by performing the occasional contract killing, the nature of what the woman had wanted with Linc didn't much concern Ringer.

What did was the fact that now five days later, his bike was still parked outside The Wolf Den, nobody having seen or heard a word from him.

Offering to pay a handsome fee if the Wolves could finish the transaction that Linc left behind, Ringer had accepted. Not so much because of the money, but because in completing the task, he would also gain access to whoever had likely done in their brother.

An eventuality they cannot, and will not, abide.

In what was supposed to be a simple act, he had sent Byrdie and Ringer. That's where things had gone sideways, two of his better men having arrived back hours later, one of them beaten badly, the target still very much alive.

"No," Snapper says. "Last check-in was twenty minutes ago. They're on the house, but nobody's come back."

Grunting, Ringer nods. It makes sense. The target is an elderly woman that doesn't speak a word of English. Having witnessed what happened, she is likely in the wind, making their task infinitely more difficult.

A fact that every man around the table knows. It doesn't need to be pointed out.

"Have them stay on it," Ringer says. "And if they get tired, send somebody else. Sooner or later, these guys have to circle back."

He doesn't know that, not for sure anyway, but it beats the alternative of doing nothing. Right now, all they have is an address and a description, a name that may or may not be real.

Where to even start looking for someone like that, especially in a town teeming with illegals, is beyond his best guess.

"Right," Snapper grunts. He adds a nod, the strain on his features matching that of the men to either side.

"And the two men?" Ringer asks, alluding to the pair that had taken on Byrdie and Gamer. "Anything?"

"Not yet," Snapper replies, "but it's a basic neighborhood. Pretty quiet right now."

This time, it is Ringer's turn to nod. If anything is going to happen, if anyone is going to return, it won't be until first light, when they have the added protection of having plenty of witnesses around.

Until then, all they can do is sit and wait.

"Any word from the woman?" Snapper asks, the conversation having devolved to just the two of them, the others sitting in silent shame on either end.

He doesn't use the woman's name, nobody but Ringer even knowing it, but he doesn't need to. Everything started with her arrival the afternoon before, will likely revolve around her until things were done.

"Not yet," Ringer replies. "I called twice, but it's four in the morning. Bitch is probably asleep."

Chapter Four

ELSA TELLER IS NOT a dog person. Or a cat person. Or a fish person. Or a believer that a person should ever willingly invite an animal into their home.

Perhaps this belief is based on her own upbringing, her father forbidding it, barely tolerating her making even the tiniest of messes as a young child. Maybe it is the schedule she keeps and the realization that she will never be able to provide a pet with the time and attention they need.

Or, more likely, it is the utter repulsion she feels at the mere thought of having to pick up animal feces or be held captive by the wants and needs of another living thing.

Leaning against the front hood of her Audi, those assorted thoughts and many others like it float through Teller's mind. Standing with one arm folded across her chest, the other is cocked near the side of her head, morning coffee already in hand.

Despite the first rays of dawn just appearing over the horizon, her face is largely hidden behind mirrored sunglasses. A thin shawl is draped over her shoulders, providing the added warmth that the sleeveless black dress and pumps she wears is lacking.

For most, the time of day would be an exercise in agony, especially given the late hour she was working until the night before. Teller barely notices as she sips at her coffee, the three hours of sleep she got a standard allotment for someone in her line of work.

What wasn't is the place she is now looking out across, a small dog park on the edge of Mira Mesa. A full city block in length, where many would see a nice swath of grass, a place for children and animals to play, she sees only wasted opportunity.

In a town with the housing market of San Diego, that one piece of ground could hold more than a half-dozen homes, easily topping over five million in total value.

The choice of meeting location is one she could do without, though admittedly there are precious few places private enough to have the type of conversation she is about to. Coffee shops make for great set pieces on television, but in reality they are filled with bored people there for no other reason than to eavesdrop and people watch.

Teller has even less time for them than she does the furry critter currently bounding her way.

Short and fluffy, the dog is charcoal in color save a few strips of white around the mouth and eyes. A pink tongue extends down over his bottom lip as he bounds along, his back end swinging from side to side, pulled along by the wagging stub of a tail.

Stopping just short of her, it presents itself at her feet, waiting for affection of some sort, before realizing there is none to be had and turning back toward its owner.

The woman Teller is actually there to speak with.

"Buddy!" the woman scolds, waddling her way across the grass. "Leave her alone."

Not bothering to voice that she seconds that opinion, Teller remains pressed flush against the side of the car. She watches as the dog bounds back toward its owner, circling her feet twice, his entire body wriggling with excitement.

"I'm so sorry," the woman says, coming to a stop in the same spot her pet had been in a moment before. Pausing awkwardly, she lifts either hand a few inches as if she might give Teller a hug before stopping.

Teller doesn't hug. Especially when the person is carrying a green plastic sack full of dog droppings.

"He just gets excited."

The woman's name is Carmella Benitez, a contact Teller put in place more than three years before. A woman in her mid-forties, she is already dressed for work in pink scrub pants and a gray zip-up sweatshirt, her thick hair pulled back into a braid.

"Don't we all," Teller replies, barely able to mask the disdain in her voice.

"Thank you for agreeing to meet out here," Benitez says, moving straight past the subject of her pet. "I appreciate it."

"No problem," Teller answers. Compared to the stops she made the day before, this is a bit distasteful, but it could be worse.

It's not as if she has to have a hand in her purse, wrapped around the grip of her Smith & Wesson Shield 2.0 handgun, just to have a conversation.

"I wanted to stop by and ask you to keep an eye out for Fran Ogo," Teller says. "There's been a bit of a setback."

Her mouth forming into a circle, Benitez takes a moment to process. Once the information seems to align, her eyebrows rise. "Oh."

"Nothing too bad," Teller adds, "nothing for you to be concerned with, but if she shows up, give me a call."

For most of the summer, the crowds had been plentiful. Not Fenway plentiful, with fans waiting outside on Yawkey Way, clamoring to get inside, but certainly enough to fill the majority of the seats at McCoy Stadium. Every night they would show up, bringing with them the sort of energy and excitement that only a minor league crowd could provide.

Families with small children. Young men out to compare themselves to the players, seeing how they measure up. Local sponsors playing random games between innings, ranging from free food giveaways to asking fans to race around the bases.

The Triple-A level was billed as a place to watch the stars of tomorrow play today. Just a phone call away from the big club up the road in Boston, that was conceivably true.

But there was something different to it as well.

Something that made it far and away the most fun I had ever had playing baseball.

The sun was just beginning to set as I pushed off the top step of the dugout and headed for my spot in left field. A smattering of applause followed me as we took the field for the start of the third, up a pair after posting one in each of the first two innings.

Overhead, the sun was sitting just a few inches above the horizon, promising the banks of stanchion lights overlooking the field would be up and active soon enough. Just after Labor Day, already sunset was beginning to creep forward, the first tiny hints of a chilly breeze popping up from time to time.

Before long, the infamous New England winter would be back, taking summer and baseball away for another year.

And taking me back to Corvallis, an eventuality I could not wait for.

Hopping over the third base line, I jogged out to the spot I had patrolled for the past two months, ever since getting called up from Double-A. Starting the season with a hot hand, I had quickly ascended the ranks, even riding it for my first few weeks in Pawtucket.

In the time since, things had cooled somewhat, though by any stretch of the definition, the season had been a success. So much so that there were some whispers that I might even get invited to spring training with the big club.

Nobody thought I had a shot at making the team just yet, but it would be a solid sign for the future just to be on the same field, an announcement that I had arrived, would be sticking around for as long as they let me.

Reaching the spot of thin grass that denoted where I usually stood, I turned toward center field. A moment later, a long, looping throw came sailing in, my friend Bryce chucking a ball over, keeping us loose.

Catching it easily, I returned it back his way, the movement smooth and easy, one I had done a thousand times before. Back and forth we went through a half-dozen throws each, interrupted only by the voice of the ancient PA announcer, a local institution that had been calling games since before I was born.

"Now batting for Scranton-Wilkes, catcher, Rich Chatman."

Shifting to the side, I underhanded the ball toward the dugout, sending it bouncing twice before being scooped up by our batboy, a young kid in a Pawtucket Red Sox uniform that was at least two sizes too big.

Behind him, vendors hawked peanuts and popcorn, sodas and hot dogs, their voices carrying through the warm fall air.

One day soon, I hoped to get the call. I hoped that the Red Sox needed me to come and patrol left field for them, standing before the mythical Green Monster, feeding off the energy of forty thousand rabid fans.

But for the time being, I was content. I missed Mira and my mama and all the other things that I had left behind, but if I couldn't be with the ones I loved, at least I got to do something I loved.

And minor league baseball for me was a love, of that there was no denying.

Pulling my cap low on my forehead, I focused on the mound. Throwing for us was a big lefty, a farm kid from Kentucky with a wicked accent and even more wicked slider. Arriving just a few weeks prior, he'd moved up the ranks faster than anybody in the organization, a virtual lock to be gone by the start of spring.

But for the time being, we were enjoying having him around, a veritable ace on the hill.

At the plate, the catcher for Scranton-Wilkes settled in, getting into his batting stance. Swinging the barrel forward a couple of times, he coiled himself tight, waiting as the pitcher went into his windup.

Rocking back, he cocked his knee toward his chest before driving forward, flinging the ball at the plate.

Wasting no time, Chatman stepped into it, stabbing the barrel of the bat at the ball. Making square contact, the ball leapt off the end of it, a low liner charging hard for the dreaded triangle between myself, the shortstop, and center field.

"Shit," I muttered, pushing off my back foot and sprinting forward. Arms pumping, I watched as the ball hung suspended, easily clearing the infield, headed hard for the open patch of grass to my left.

Sprinting with everything I had, I tracked it through the air, closing the gap between us, my singular focus on getting to the spot before the ball did. Air seized tight in my chest, a low grunt escaped my lips as I pounded out three more hard steps before launching myself through the air.

Extended parallel to the ground, I stretched as far as my body would allow, arm at full length, my obliques and serratus muscles straining to give me one extra inch.

The webbing of my glove sagged just slightly as the ball slammed home. The crowd erupted on cue, the sound there and gone as I came crashing to the ground, my full weight landing on my outstretched shoulder.

In such a vulnerable position, there was no way to brace myself, no chance of breaking the fall as I hit hard, sliding a few feet before coming to a stop.

Just as there was no way to deny the popping sound that it had made when I landed.

Or the agony that traveled my entire left side, my arm limp as I lay on my stomach, gasping for air.

Chapter Five

"I'm sorry I called and woke you," I say, glancing across to Jeff Swinger. I then roll my glance over to Emily Stapleton and add, "And I'm sorry he called and woke you."

In response, Swinger raises a hand, waving off the comment. Beside him, Stapleton stares my way.

"The next time you apologize, I'm going to hit you," she says. "Just like the next time you *don't* call me, I'm going to hit you."

I can feel my eyebrows rise slightly at the statement, easily the most aggressive I can ever remember her making. Rocking back an inch, I glance over, just long enough to show my surprise and to receive the fact that she isn't kidding.

Understood.

"I said the same thing to him not two hours ago," Angelique adds, stepping up along the side of us, turning our trio into a quartet. Huddled into a small cluster, we are still tucked into the corner of the Paradise Valley cafeteria, though the onset of morning means our time here is fast coming to a close.

Already, bleary-eyed doctors preparing for the backend of a double shift have started shuffling in, looking for their jolt of liquid caffeine. At any moment, eager young interns will start filing through, ready to get their day started.

And with them will come every possible permutation in between, from hospital staff to concerned family members needing somewhere else to be.

Which means we now need somewhere else to be as well.

For much of the last hour and a half, the group has sat motionless, enduring a stilted conversation that still leaves quite a bit to be delved into. Some basic questions have been answered, but just as many more remain.

We are all tired and frustrated, feeling the strain of the last week, of the truncated timetable we now have inside the hospital.

Glancing to each of the people in our small group, I can see each of them staring intently back at me. Meeting them one at a time, I raise my palms, conceding the point they are trying to make.

"Okay, I get it. We're all in this together. Nothing happens without at least somebody else knowing about it."

Right now, that is the best I can do. The situation seems to be evolving too fast, the disparate directions too many, to ever keep everyone completely apprised.

Just like earlier, it wasn't that I was excluding Stapleton, it was that I only had time to make one phone call.

And it wasn't like I didn't know Swinger would instantly call her anyway.

"Speaking of which, it would probably be best if you guys both gave Angelique your phone numbers," I add, my friends each nodding in agreement.

Beside me, Angelique presses her lips into a tight line, the closest we're going to get to a straight affirmation.

Turning at the waist, I leave the logistical discussion behind, shifting my focus to the pair of women behind us. After the night we've all been through, they both wear it plainly on their features, Valerie appearing concerned, her grandmother exhausted.

Staring at them, I wish there is something I can tell them to make it easier. Some promise of things being okay. A bit of optimism to help them get past the combined shock of Mira's passing and people showing up at their door with ill intentions.

But I know just as surely, I can't. Even trying to would be bullshit, an attempt more to make myself feel better than of actually helping them.

None of us know how to handle what is happening at the moment.

Probably won't for quite some time.

"Moving on, I think the bigger question right now is what to do with these two," I say. Shifting back to the group, I make sure my voice is lowered, seeing as Angelique and Stapleton both glance back to the table.

"The house is out," Swinger says, beginning with the most obvious. "The Wolves will still be looking for them."

He's right, on both points. They definitely already have a name and address on the Ogo's. My visit with Hiram might have put them off for the time being, but it won't be enough to make them stop.

Somehow, they don't seem the sort. Especially not after what happened last night.

"Mine too," I say. "They already had my wife's name, tossed our house. If they haven't figured out who I am yet, it's only a matter of time."

Nobody bothers reacting to this. Like Swinger, I'm just snatching at the easy stuff, getting it out of the way.

"What about my place?" Angelique offers. "We have plenty of space."

She doesn't add that is because her husband and daughter are both gone. That her son is now also out of the house, residing in a room not a hundred yards from where we're standing. Or that putting a young woman like Valerie in the space that was once Mira's will likely be extremely difficult.

But she doesn't have to. Because we all already understand it, and for those reasons, there's no way I would ever let that happen.

"Thanks," I say, "but-"

"And this is San Diego," Angelique adds, "even if they did somehow know my last name, there are thousands of Martinez's in the area. They'd never be able to check on them all."

Both points are accurate, but it doesn't matter. Of all the feelings that have permeated my thinking in the last week, the one that stings the most, lingers the longest, is the notion that I didn't protect my wife. I had a responsibility. I even had an inkling something wasn't right, and I suppressed it.

And because of that, she is gone.

There is not a chance in hell I'm running a similar risk with her mother, this woman being one of a very small handful left in the world that I can consider family.

No matter how many times she offers.

"I'm actually thinking someplace even a little further out," I say.

"The place where you're staying," Swinger says, jumping ahead.

"Yeah," I reply, nodding grimly. "Little concrete dive out in the middle of nowhere. One other room is used, and I'm pretty sure that's by the owner."

Swinger raises his eyebrows slightly, an unspoken signal that he might not be in love with the idea, but he sees the merit in it.

"Very quiet," I add. "We'll be able to hear a motorcycle engine – or anything else for that matter – coming for miles."

Glancing to Stapleton and Angelique, I can see from the unease on their faces they aren't crazy about the notion, but like myself, they don't have another suggestion right now either.

We have devolved into what the Navy calls a strictly touch situation. A point in time when underwater where things become so dark, all we can do is inch along, feeling with our hands, piecing together things as best we can.

I don't like any of this, but it's all we have.

"Okay," Angelique says, "but there's just one more problem you need to figure out first."

"What's that?"

Turning her head toward the table, she takes in the two women, their defensive postures, the lowered din of their voices as they sit deep in conversation.

"Convincing them to go with you."

Chapter Six

DETECTIVE MALCOLM MARSH stands in the living room of his condo in Imperial Beach staring out through the picture window that comprises the entire western side of the spread. Sitting right on the coast, there is nothing between him and the water save a pane of glass, a thin concrete walkway, and fifty yards of sand. Grains of the latter still cling to his ankles and calves as he stands with a bottle of water in hand, using a towel to wipe away beads of perspiration from the top of his smooth head.

Already stripped free of the fleece he'd been wearing, he can feel the cool morning air passing through the crack at the bottom of the window, picking at the perspiration on his skin. His eyes pinched tight against the glow of the rising sun dancing off the water, he looks without really seeing, processing things in his mind.

The condo in Imperial Beach is nice. At over a thousand square feet, it is spacious, sits right on the water, has a phenomenal view. Most people in the city would kill for a place like it. Or to even rent a room like one of his.

But it isn't La Jolla. Isn't even Del Mar or Solana Beach or one of the other spots further up the coast. The sorts of places that raise eyebrows, people instantly knowing what is meant when he says he lives on the waterfront in one of those towns.

That he is someone important, somebody doing quite well for himself.

A black man in his mid-thirties, Marsh is on a trajectory. Working as a detective and owning the home he now stands in are solid foundations, they are directly in line with where he's supposed to be right now, but they aren't the end goal.

Not by a long shot.

Glancing to the clock on the wall, Marsh steps away from the window. His pupils dilate as he leaves behind the bright sun, tiny pops of light lingering behind his eyelids with each blink. Stepping across his living room, he goes straight for the coffee table and takes up his cellphone.

"One minute after seven, he'll be up," Marsh whispers.

Having not the slightest doubt, he scrolls through his recent call history, finding the number he is looking for and pressing send. A moment later, he hears it connect as ringing begins.

Working out of the Central District of the San Diego Police Department, there is never a shortage of things to keep a detective busy. Assigned to the late-afternoon and evening shift, rarely is there a time when there isn't an altercation, a drug bust, a domestic violence dispute, or a dozen other things to keep him occupied.

Every day, he shows up, prepared to diligently work his way through them. Dressed in a suit, perfectly coiffed, he is more skilled than most in how to play the game. Knows perfectly well that perception often matters much more than reality. That plugging away, even in a place as seemingly desperate as the Central District, will one day get him noticed.

But there's nothing wrong with keeping an eye out for something that might help speed things along.

Something like the shooting of Mira Clady in Balboa Park a few days prior.

The phone rings nearly a half-dozen times before it is picked up. There is no immediate response over the line, nothing but a few heavy breaths, the sound of the freeway running beneath tires audible in the background.

"Hello?" Marsh asks.

"Who is this?" a male voice responds. Wariness plain, the man sounds exhausted, as if he has been awake all night.

Warning flags begin to wave in Marsh's mind, as bright and unmistakable as fireworks in the night sky.

"This is Detective Malcolm Marsh. Is this Kyle Clady?"

Another heavy breath is heard, this one more of an exhalation. "Good morning, Detective. How are you?"

"Are you..." Marsh begins before pulling back to start anew. "Is everything okay?"

"Yeah," Clady replies. "Just tired. Couldn't sleep. You understand."

Marsh himself can't. He's never lost someone especially close to him, has none of the moral qualms that plague some of his coworkers.

Everyday, he goes to work, does everything he can for the people of San Diego. And every night, he returns home and sleeps easily, leaving it all behind until the next shift.

The fact that he is now even thinking about Mira Clady, is reaching out to her husband, speaks more to the possibilities the case presents for him personally than any attachment to it professionally.

"I do," Marsh replies, "and I apologize for calling so early, but my partner and I received some news last night that couldn't wait."

The *news* he is speaking of can definitely be attributed more to his partner's insistence on checking every camera throughout Balboa Park, though now that it has presented itself, Marsh is not about to let it pass.

The perks of being the lead detective.

"The blanket," Clady replies.

"No," Marsh replies, "that is still at our lab undergoing forensic analysis. I've asked that it be fast-tracked, but in a city the size of San Diego..."

This time it is his turn to leave the end of a statement dangling, presupposing that Clady will pick up where he is going with it. As a Navy SEAL, he should have been through more than his share of dealing with bureaucracy.

"We were able to pull an image from one of the cameras on the other side of the park," Marsh says. "Taken just a few minutes after the incident, it looks like it could be the guy you described."

He doesn't bother pointing out that they ran the man through the system, already tracking down a name and an extensive criminal history. Those types of things will wait for later, when Marsh can get Clady into the precinct, watching him receive the news personally.

On the other end of the line, there is no response. Nothing more than terse breathing, the sort of thing Marsh would expect.

"Can I get you to swing by the precinct later this morning and see if you can identify the man?"

Chapter Seven

THE OGO LADIES were absolutely insistent on two things upon our arrival to the Valley View Inn & Suites, the sorely misnamed motel that has been my home for the last five nights. A decision having nothing to do with amenities, or proximity, or even recommendation from another living soul, I myself ended up there because it is a long way from my actual home.

The one I bought and shared with my wife. The same place I now can't set foot in without being reminded of some new tiny aspect of her, something I haven't thought about in ages.

Like the way she loved wearing my old threadbare sweatshirts around the house, nothing but tan legs sticking out the bottom. Or the smell of her shampoo. The specific brand of tea she liked to drink.

To say nothing of a million other things, all threatening to reduce me to tears without warning.

Pulling up in front of the dusty low-slung structure, all concrete and faded paint, I could see the expressions on their faces. Mirroring my own from a few days earlier, they each stared forward, practically seeing the camera crew for a low-budget horror movie starting to set up before making their demands.

One, they would be staying in the same room together. Two, they would be paying for that room themselves.

The first, I had fully expected. Fran's lack of English proficiency, the scene at their house the night before, the fact that they barely knew me, was all enough for them to want the added security of being together.

The second point surprised me, but after the argument that had ensued in the hospital cafeteria over whether they were coming at all or not, I knew better than to object. In that first instance, I had only managed to come out on top through the help of my friends and mother-in-law. This time, I wasn't nearly as well equipped, content to let them make any requests they wanted.

Just so long as they stay here, tucked away and safe from the Wolves or whoever else might be looking for them. The list of things on my plate is plenty long already without needing to play bodyguard as well, the call I'd received on the way out just one more thing.

The morning sun is barely above the horizon as we step away from the front office. Shining bright from the east, it lands flush against my right side, that eye closing tight to keep it at bay. Already, the threat of a warm day is at hand, none of us saying a word as we head across the parking lot toward the opposite arm of the motel sprawl.

As in the days before, the only two cars in the lot belong to the live-in manager and myself, the old guy barely lifting an eyebrow as I walked in with the mismatched duo at half past seven in the morning and asked for the room closest to mine with two beds in it.

I guess doing what he does, in the place where is, there isn't a lot he hasn't seen.

Without the burden of luggage or personal effects, moving in is easy, as simple as walking to the door and turning the key. Reaching it first, Valerie does the honors, pushing the front open and peering inside.

"Home sweet home," she mutters, a dour expression crossing her face as she steps to the side. She waits as her grandmother turns and offers me a tight-lipped smile, her head dipping slightly, the universal symbol for silent thanks.

Returning the gesture, I watch as she turns and disappears within, swallowed up by a den of stale air and furnishings last manufactured when she was my age.

A few feet away, Valerie waits until her grandmother is inside before leaning in and grasping the door handle. Pulling it just an inch short of closed, she takes a few steps my direction, closing the gap to less than a foot. Her arms folded, she lowers her voice and says, "You know we can't stay here forever. I have a job, class. Nana has appointments."

I know all of that. Every bit of it she shared earlier, her tone noticeably more intense. Still, that doesn't mean she isn't right.

This isn't a permanent solution, by any stretch of the imagination.

"You won't have to," I reply. "This is just to buy us a bit of time until we can figure out what's going on."

Glancing up at me, Valerie swallows hard before shifting her focus back out to the parking lot. On her face is a look I've seen hundreds of times before, standard response for a person's first exposure to peril.

Once upon a time, I'm certain I wore the same exact expression.

The world today is set up to insulate a person, to provide them with every creature comfort imaginable, wrapping them in a cocoon of familiarity. A person doesn't have to drive if they don't want to. They don't have to cook if they'd rather not. They don't even need to go to Wal-Mart if they so choose. Everything is just a button click away.

Having those sorts of services, living in a society so heavily trafficked by rules and procedures and enforcement, inculcates people to the realities of life. It makes them forget that evil still exists, that most are more vulnerable than ever.

Doing what I do for a living, it's been a long, long time since I had even an inkling of such a bubble. For Valerie, hers was just shattered, ripped apart by the pair of men that stormed through her door.

And unfortunately for her, never again will she be able to rebuild it.

"You okay?" I ask.

Flicking her gaze back to me, she nods. I can tell there are things on her mind, questions she wants to ask, but to her credit, they remain tucked away. Why that is, I can't say, but I don't press it.

Right now, I'm going through the process of grieving my wife in probably the most abnormal way possible. I'm in no position to tell her how to process things.

"Later on, we'll run to the store," I say. "Get you guys some toiletries, clothes, whatever you need."

Again, she nods. She swallows once more, a lump traveling the length of her throat, before she asks, "So what happens now?"

"Now?" I ask. "Now, you wait here."

"I got that," she snaps back, a bit of her original personality shining through the trauma of the last eight hours. "I mean, for what? What are you planning to do?"

Matching her glance, I look away, peering across the parking lot, imagining the freeway in the distance. Already backing up with the start of another workday, I can practically see cars sitting nose-to-tail, filled with people growing increasingly agitated as bleary eyes fade and caffeine kicks in.

My plans have been a fairly liquid thing for almost a week now. There is no blueprint for what I'm going through, no way to plan for it, to even wrap my head around it.

If there were, my brother-in-law damned sure wouldn't be laying in a hospital bed right now.

"Traffic is too thick to bother heading in town," I say. "So I'm going to rack out for a couple of hours. Then I'll head in, talk to Detective Marsh, take a look at whatever he found."

After that, depending on how good his information is, I'll make a quick decision on whether to follow that angle or go find the doctor the Ogo's mentioned earlier.

"You need a hand?" she asks.

I appreciate the offer, but the best thing she can do is stay with her grandmother. Stay inside. Remain as hidden as possible.

Which won't be hard in a place as decrepit as the Valley View.

"I'll give a call if I do."

Chapter Eight

A COUPLE HOURS turned in to just less than three, which was more than I intended but infinitely less than I needed. Just long enough to go through one full REM cycle, by the time my conscious mind came back to the surface, pulling images of my Mira, and her shooter, and Balboa Park, and everything else that seemed to lurk just beneath the surface like some sort of perverse memory shark back to the fore, I knew that even attempting any further rest was futile.

Not with my mind back to buzzing along, pushing through everything that happened, everything that still lays ahead.

Rising and making my way to the bathroom, I inspected my face in the mirror, seeing the results of the night before etched plainly across my face. My left cheekbone looked to be distended more than half an inch, as if someone had spliced a golf ball in half and shoved it under my skin. In the center of it was the inverted crescent where the surface had broken, stubby ends of the stitches protruded like the legs of a spider.

Already, several shades of black and purple colored the area, the total span encompassing a diameter of more than an inch and a half. Reaching all the way over to the corner of my eye, I could see a splash of red along the bottom, broken blood vessels plain to see.

Having had enough bruises in my day to know how the general progression goes, it would be a week or more before things returned to normal. Much too long to put off the detective, and much too large to even try covering it, I jumped in the shower, letting the warmest water the place possessed wash over me for a few minutes.

Once my muscles were loosened and I was feeling quasi-close to human again, I dressed and jumped in the car, no sign of the Ogo women as I went.

A half-hour later, I now find myself sitting back in front of the Central District precinct. Wanting even less to be here than I did a few days ago, I sit and stare up at the building, considering my options, trying to determine if there is any way I can get around this.

By nearly every calculation, there is not. Since the incident first happened, Detective Marsh has been looking for some reason to pin things on me. If I blow him off now, he'll figure something is up. He'll look at me closer. And I can't have that.

As far as he knows, I've done nothing wrong. I damned sure didn't harm my wife, but I can't quite say the same for her killer. If I don't at least show up and go through the motions of trying to help identify him, it will be a red flag.

And I've got too much left to do to afford one of those right now.

Stepping out of the car, I pause for a pair of kids on motorized scooters to fly past, neither even glancing my way, before heading to the front door. The same young man with black skin and close-cropped hair is working the desk as I enter, his features crinkling slightly as he sees the side of my face.

"Good morning," he says. "Can I help you?"

We had this exact exchange four days prior, though I don't bother pointing it out. No doubt he sees dozens of people every day, none any more memorable than the last.

Besides, right now, all he is seeing is the goose egg protruding from my cheek.

"I'm here to speak with Detective Marsh," I say. Anticipating the next statement, I add, "He called earlier and said he would be in, asked me to stop by."

Pausing, the young man nods, working through what I told him, his immediate response no doubt stifled. Shifting to the right, he lifts the phone from his desk and mutters a few words before returning it to its cradle.

"He'll be right out."

Chapter Nine

"Good God Almighty!" The words are out before the guy has even fully entered the room, a hand rising to his chin. Stepping over the threshold, he pauses, pulling his fist back a few inches and bending at the waist to inspect my face. "What the hell happened to you?"

Saying nothing, I remained motionless in my seat. Back in the same interview suite we had used over the weekend, I am sitting with my chair turned parallel to the metal table in the center, my arm from the elbow down resting atop it.

Arching an eyebrow, I look to Marsh sitting at the head of the table. Dressed in a suit that must have cost a minimum four figures, a cup of equally overpriced coffee sits before him, the smell permeating the room.

On his face is an expression of agitation, not bothering to turn toward the sound of the voice entering behind him.

"Mr. Clady," he says, "this is my partner, Mark Tinley. He was out of the country when we met on Saturday. He's been working the case with me since his return."

The guy is roughly the same age as me, though in a lot of ways he reminds me of the young recruits that pour into the base in equal batches every so often. Young and fit, he exudes unfounded confidence, the type that being able to wear a uniform instills, having not yet experienced the polar opposite end of the job thus far.

He will, no doubt, but not quite yet.

Stepping inside, he closes the door behind him. He drops a file down on the table beside Marsh before leaning across, extending a hand my way, "Detective Mark Tinley, SDPD."

Much like his partner on our first meeting, he insists on using his full extended title, a classic power move that I am in no mood for.

Making zero effort to rise, I accept the shake and reply, "Petty Officer Kyle Clady, United States Navy."

Nodding slightly, he takes the chair exactly across from me, Marsh waiting for him to settle before turning his attention back my way. "Welcome, Detective, we were actually just discussing what happened to his face."

He pauses long enough to let me know the floor is mine, that an unspoken question has been asked. In no way do I want to answer, to give them even the slightest hint of a response, but I can't afford to be openly antagonistic either.

My face is clearly marred. I am a trained SEAL. And just a few nights earlier I was very nearly arrested for assaulting one of the paramedics that arrived to help my wife.

"Haven't been able to sleep," I reply, "so a couple of nights, I went over to the base to work in the ring. Some were better than others."

Knowing it was best to leave the answer as short as possible, that the fewer details there are to keep straight the better, I stop there.

Even at that, the sheer disbelief on Marsh's features is palpable. "And neither of you wore gloves?"

Without glancing down, I know he is referencing the scabs covering the knuckles on my right hand. First put there in the desert a few nights before, they were reopened just a dozen hours earlier by the unexpected intruders at the Ogo's.

Matching his gaze for a moment, I keep my features neutral. I let him see that the questions don't bother me, that I'm not scrambling for a response, before replying, "Sometimes, you want the pain. Was kind of hoping it would help me sleep."

"Did it?" Tinley asks, my gaze lingering on Marsh before rolling over toward his partner.

"No," I reply, "still keep seeing that bastard's face every time I close my eyes." Shifting back to Marsh, I say, "Which is why you asked me here today, correct?"

Again, Marsh employs his annoying habit of pausing before responding. He waits, as if trying to assert his control over the moment, making sure every other person is looking his way, before nodding. Shifting his focus to the table, he slides over the folder that Tinley had placed beside him.

Drawing it into the space between us, he keeps all five fingertips pressed down atop it, his palm tented upward in the middle. "Like I mentioned on the phone, we were able to pull some images from a camera on the opposite side of the park. Six minutes prior to the 911 call, this man was spotted coming out of the canyon between the Municipal Gym and the Air and Space Museum."

I don't know the park nearly as well as my wife or her family, but I've been around enough to know the landmarks. The two buildings he's alluding to are on the opposite side of Park Boulevard from where we were, at most a quarter mile from the spot Mira was shot.

The last I saw of the guy that night, he was running off in that direction. Moving at even a moderate pace, the timeline fit.

My stomach draws tight, adrenaline seeping into my system, as my focus moves down to the folder. Waiting, I watch as Marsh grabs the top flap and draws it back, revealing a single black-and-white photograph.

Using the pads of his middle and index fingers, he slides it to the side, revealing an enhanced copy of the previous one. Filling in the grainy pixels, a glossy veneer covers it, making the image at least three times as clear as the original.

Not that I needed it, the first being more than enough to confirm.

All air ceases to enter or exit my lungs as I lean forward at the waist. Warmth creeps to my face, along my back, as I stare at the image.

There is no doubt the man is who I first met that night. The man whose carcass is currently serving as coyote chow in an unmarked cabin out in the desert thanks to me and my friends.

But that doesn't stop the image from gripping me tight, every physiological response I have spiking in concert.

"Who is he?" I mutter.

"Is that him?" Marsh asks, ignoring my question.

I don't take my eyes from the page. Not because I know what they're expecting and want to play the part, but because again I can't begin to tamp down the anger roiling through me.

"One hundred percent," I reply.

"Guy's name is Mark Lincoln," Tinley says, an admission I can tell instantly was never meant to be shared.

Extending a hand out to the side, Marsh cuts him off, slapping at the table in front of his partner. "And he is a person of interest right now."

Looking at the photo one extra second, juxtaposing it with the last I saw of the man, his lifeless body propped in a chair, I move back in my seat. I work to keep my face clear of reaction, shifting my glance between them.

"Meaning what?"

"Meaning we will bring him in for questioning, begin to build a case," Marsh said.

There will be no questioning, no case, but I don't bother saying as much. The longer they stay on that path, the more freedom I have to do what I need to elsewhere.

"Okay," I say, shoving out a sigh, a sound mixed of grief and frustration. "Thanks for calling me in. Glad to know there's some movement."

Flipping the folder closed, Marsh draws it back toward himself. He keeps his fingers pressed down into it, staring at me, before saying, "Of course. We'll be sure to do the same if anything else comes up."

Chapter Ten

A FEW YEARS north of forty and a few pounds north of two-forty, Ringer would ballpark the number of cheeseburgers he'd had in his life at a thousand or more. No exaggeration, no excessive hyperbole, just simple math. Once a week or so for at least the last twenty years put things right at the number, which was conservative to say the least.

Of those, some were better than others. Just like some beer was better than others. And some sex was better than others.

But at the end of the day, by and large, they were all just burgers. Meat, cheese, bun.

Which was why he had never understood the California fascination with In-N-Out Burger. A transplant himself, he had called the state home for most of his cheeseburger-eating adult life, only trying it a handful of times.

All were decent, but not spectacular. And certainly not worth sitting and waiting upwards of a half-hour for.

Parked in the back of the Mission Hills franchise lot, the thought again goes through his head as he walks past the line of cars filling the drive-thru. Wrapping around the side and back of the building, it contains everything from rusted pickups to shiny BMW's, all full of people looking to get their lunch fix.

Meanwhile a Wendy's sits across the road, almost empty.

Shaking his head slightly, Ringer walks past the side entrance into the place. His gait long and slow, he spots who he is looking for sitting on an outdoor table at the far front edge of the property, alone beneath an umbrella's shade. With no food of any kind on the table, she sits with her bag beside her, phone in hand.

Glancing through the front glass of the establishment, he sees a couple of people immediately look away, standard practice for someone with his appearance.

Which is kind of the point.

Giving no indication that he even noticed, Ringer walks on to the front table. He makes sure to drag his boot heels to announce his presence before arriving, stopping alongside the table and folding his arms, staring down at Elsa Teller.

Without looking up from her phone, she says, "I heard that monstrosity you rode in on pull up five minutes ago. What took so long?"

"Damned place is packed clear out to the road," Ringer says. "Why the hell did you pick this spot?"

Staying silent a moment, Teller finishes her business on the phone, pressing a flurry of buttons, before shoving it into the bag beside her. Offering a frosty smile, she says, "Because it's packed clear out to the road."

Unfolding his arms, Ringer steps to the side, sliding in on the bench seat of the pre-fab picnic table. Galvanized steel coated in rubber, it was designed for someone half his size, the rigid construction biting into his legs.

He doesn't react in any way. With luck, he'll be gone before it even matters.

"What happened to the lady with all the sand I met yesterday?" Ringer asks.

"That lady was there to offer a business proposal," Teller says. "Now that we have come to an agreement, I figured somewhere a bit more neutral would be in order."

His eyes hidden behind thick sunglasses, Ringer casts a glance to the window. In it, he can see their reflection, aware of how odd the pairing might look, the perfect cover for what she is describing.

A day before, she had shown up with a hand shoved into her purse, gripping a handgun the entire time. Now, she is protected by the masses, tons of curious onlookers with cameras and phones and whatever else on hand.

"We ran into a problem," Ringer opens. Even as he says the words, he hates the way they taste, even more how they sound.

"How bad?" she asks.

Exhaling slowly, Ringer says, "My guys went to Ogo's last night. Somebody else was there, and it got ugly."

If the woman is surprised in the least, she offers nothing to give it away. What can be seen of her features remain neutral, her voice even. "Deaths?"

"No," Ringer says, "but the old woman is in the wind."

Offering nothing for several seconds, Teller reaches up and slides her sunglasses halfway down her nose. She looks over the edge of them at Ringer, letting her disbelief show plainly. "I'm sorry, one *old woman* was able to get past you guys?"

Ringer's hands curl up into fists at the statement, oversized ham hocks lying in the center of the table. Veins stand out the length of his arms, jutting beneath tanned skin and heavy ink.

Leaving them there, he says, "No. She wasn't alone, which is why I called you."

The sunglasses remain perched on the bridge of Teller's nose. "She wasn't alone, so you called me?"

It is clear the woman is just messing with him, trying to get under his skin. Under any other circumstances, he would reach across the table. He would wrap his hand around her delicate neck, grinding his fingers and thumb down into the nerves on either side of it.

And once she was out, he would have some fun.

"There were two of them," he says. "One big and heavy. Soft, like a lawyer or something."

Her eyebrows twitch slightly at this, though she says nothing.

"The other smaller, in shape, a good fighter. May or may not be a veteran. You know anybody like that?"

The entire conversation is so far beneath Ringer, he can barely contain his ire to sit through it. Sitting and staring at the woman, he hates that his guys messed up, even more that he's now forced to go through this charade as a result.

At this point, though, one of his members is likely dead and another got beaten badly. There is no walking away from this, no task that is too great to bear.

Using her middle finger, Teller slides her glasses back into position. She rises from her seat, collects her purse, and looks down at Ringer. "Let me make some calls. I'll get back to you."

Glancing to the empty table between them, Ringer's brows come together slightly. "What, that's it? You're not even going to eat?"

"Here?" she replies, her head rocking back slightly with a smirk. "No way in hell I'm waiting in that line. It's just a damn burger."

―――――

The decision to have surgery wasn't really much of a decision. Not if I ever wanted to have a pain-free existence, not having to worry about aches or clicking or any of an assortment of ailments that baseball players experience later in their lives. And certainly not if I ever wanted to resume playing baseball again.

The official diagnosis was a dislocated shoulder with a torn rotator cuff, which was the polite way of saying that I had basically destroyed any sort of connective tissue in one of the most important joints in my body. Time and again I had tried to discuss other options – whether they be acupuncture, therapy, or Chinese medicine – with the doctor, but after my fifth or sixth inquiry he finally shut me down.

Forget playing baseball. If ever I wanted to have a fully-functional, twenty-three-year-old shoulder again, I had no choice but to go under the knife.

But that didn't make it any easier.

Sitting in the small holding area, my left leg rocked incessantly.

Extended out before me on the hospital bed I was sitting on, it was bare from the mid-thigh down, the paper gown I was given not nearly long enough for my frame.

On my left side, a nurse fussed about, inserting a main line IV into the crook of my arm. Older and dowdy, her lips were pursed into a permanent frown, her brows close together behind her wire rimmed glasses.

To my opposite side was my mama, her purse in her lap, both hands clasped atop it. Trying hard not to let me see her nerves, she watched the nurse work before turning her attention my way.

"Did you hear from Mira?" she asked.

"Yeah," I replied, trying to ignore the repeated jabs the nurse was plunging into my veins, "she called before I left this morning."

"Really?" she asked. "That must have been..."

"One in the morning there," I said, having already done the math. "Poor girl sounded groggy as hell. I think she set an alarm to wake her for the call."

A thin smile crossed her face as she thought on it, before saying, "I kind of thought she would come out."

"She wanted to, and even tried to pull a few strings," I said, "but she's training with the national racquetball team in L.A. right now. If she'd have left..."

Mama nodded in understanding. "Right. Might never have gotten another shot."

"Yeah," I agreed. "And for what? To sit and stare at me all laid up? No, thanks."

I could tell there was a great many things she wanted to say in response, some of them even making it as far as her mouth dipping open, before she thought better of it. Clamping her jaw shut, she extended a hand, patting me on the forearm.

"Well, I can't begin to tell you how excited I am to do all that. Hopefully even get to hear you complain. Bring you food whenever you demand it. The works."

Beside me, the nursed snorted, a sharp, phlegmy sound that rocked her head back an inch. Hearing it, the right corner of my mouth turned up into a smile, mama's acerbic humor once again cutting the tension in the room.

Too bad it couldn't repair tendons and ligaments.

"Okay, how are you doing this morning?" a voice called, the question arriving before the asker. An instant later, the curtain separating us from others in the pre-op area was peeled back, a heavy-set man with glasses and a walrus moustache sweeping into the room.

Already dressed in scrubs, he looked like he'd been up for hours, fully-caffeinated and ready to go to work.

"Are we ready to get that shoulder fixed up?"

Chapter Eleven

I'M SO CHARGED as I step out of the Central District precinct, I can barely keep a thought in my head. Exiting the front door, I turn to the left, making it three full strides before realizing I'm parked in the opposite direction. Turning on a heel, I head back toward it, not sure how exactly I'm going to manage to drive, but thinking I have to anyway.

If for no other reason than to put distance between myself and the building. To keep Marsh from finding a window somewhere and watching my every move, trying to gauge it for what he feels is a proper reaction.

Slowing my pace, drawing in a deep breath, I head back toward my car. Using the fob, I slide inside and start the engine, sitting for a moment, feeling the vents blow warm air against my skin.

The inclusion of the name Mike Lincoln was no doubt a mistake. The second Marsh gets done watching me, he'll turn his attention to giving Tinley an ass chewing, letting it be known that disclosing such details in an active investigation isn't acceptable, even to family members.

If not for his immediate reaction at the table, I would almost feel like the admission had been planted just to see what I did next.

Starting the car, I ease away from the curb and out into traffic, looping away from the precinct. Like I told Valerie earlier, I have a next stop in the progression, the next place I plan to swing by and visit, but right now I'm still busy rolling around what I just found out in my head.

His name alone means nothing in terms of the man himself. Already I have found and eliminated that problem, leaving his body to be found by any hungry animal looking for a quick meal.

In terms of how he could relate to whatever larger scheme the Ogo's are a part of, how that all ties to my Mira, it is another big piece to what I'm looking for.

People with names have addresses. And addresses have all sorts of things in them, such as correspondence or telephone bills or anything else that might help me.

Just like these bastards tore my house apart looking for anything that might help them.

Heading toward the I-5, I don't jump on the freeway as originally planned. Instead I shoot past it, moving toward downtown, my next destination unplanned, but still highly vital.

If this were a movie, I would now call up some tech-savvy nerd in a bunker somewhere. I would give him the information I just found out, add in what I already knew, and let him go to work using his massive hand-built computer system. By the time I arrived an hour later, he would have a full working file for me, ready to pass off an information dump, acting supremely bored the entire time.

If I wasn't worried about Marsh potentially subpoenaing phones and computers at some point, I might even call one of my friends and ask them to look, or pull off the side of the road and use my own device to do some digging myself.

None of those are options, so I am going with the next best thing I can manage. Entering the financial district, I turn and head south, using the skyline as my map. Easing ahead, I keep going until I spot what I am looking for, the enormous glass and steel dome as recognizable as Petco Park or the convention center where Comic Con takes place each summer.

Hooking a right, I pull into the parking lot for the Central Library, hub of the San Diego system. Knowing that somewhere inside is a computer room the size of a lecture hall, I jump from the car and head toward the front door, barely able to keep myself to a jog.

I have Mike Lincoln's name. It's time to do some research.

Chapter Twelve

Detective Malcolm Marsh is still stewing. He hadn't held a great deal of hope for the meeting with Kyle Clady, but he was certainly expecting more than what came to pass.

Namely, that his side of the table would be the one to garner something of merit, rather than the other way around.

Seated behind his desk, he waits with his fingers laced over his stomach. The pads of his thumbs come together, tapping in a steady rhythm, his gaze focused on the door. Judging by the sounds of conversation going on out in the bullpen, the object of his ire is steadily moving his way.

Heaven forbid the guy ever make a simple trip to the bathroom without talking to every single person in the office along the way.

Feeling his impatience rise with each passing moment, Marsh sits and waits. Time and again he replays the events of the meeting in his mind, each pass through only ratcheting the agitation he feels, so much so that by the time his partner swings into the room, it is all he can do not to leap to his feet and begin yelling.

He won't, because that would be unprofessional. It would cause a scene. It would be something that coworkers would notice and remember, maybe even making it into his file as a footnote.

And someone with career aspirations can't afford footnotes.

But that doesn't mean they can't get good and pissed, just the same.

"Close the door," Marsh says the instant Tinley crosses the threshold into the room.

Thinking nothing of it, the younger man turns and swings the door shut, the heavy wood connecting firmly with the frame. Turning back, he wears a smile on his face, a lingering remnant of whatever his last conversation was before arriving.

Marsh is in no mood for it.

"What the hell were you thinking?" he asks. His voice is low and measured, enough of an edge to get his point across.

On cue, Tinley stops where he is standing, a statue frozen in the center of the narrow strip of space between their respective desks. His mouth forms into a circle, his eyes going wide, though he says nothing.

From the look on his face, he isn't quite sure exactly what Marsh is referring to.

"When do we ever – *ever* – give away information like that to family?" Marsh asks. Unlacing his hands, he leans forward, his chair squeaking slightly. Resting his elbows on the front edge of his desk, he adds, "Especially before we've had a chance to vet it ourselves?"

The response comes in two distinct parts, the first nothing more than the visual register of what he was saying, Tinley finally putting things in place. The second was for heat to come to the surface, a rosy tinge rising to his tanned face.

"Apologies," he says. "I knew the second I said it I shouldn't have."

"Damn right you shouldn't have," Marsh agrees.

"I was so used to talking about it with you at that point, I didn't realize..."

Remaining rigid, Marsh sits and stares at Tinley. Some of the angst he was feeling previously has already started to dissolve, expecting more of a fight from the younger man.

Acknowledging and apologizing isn't what he was expecting, a ploy that cut things off before they really got heated. Which is probably a good thing, making sure the conversation stayed civil, a point made without the potential charring of a bridge.

Leaning back, Marsh grunts. He nods softly, signaling they are good. They aren't quite, and he'll be much more guarded with the access he grants Tinley moving forward, but the young man doesn't need to know all that just yet.

Working with him has been an excellent exercise in what he'll undoubtedly face hundreds of times in the future. Bringing people along, molding them into what he wants and needs, is going to be a part of where he's headed.

The better he gets at it now, the easier it will be in the future.

Especially considering he still hasn't decided if Tinley will be a part of that future. His loose lips are a problem, but his appearance and affable nature could more than make up for it.

Extending a hand toward Tinley's chair, Marsh waits as the young man takes a seat.

"What kind of read did you get on Clady?"

Settling down onto his chair, Tinley raises a hand to his scalp, his fingers digging in above his ear. He ponders it a moment before replying, "Hard to say. I hadn't met him before, so I didn't see how he acted in the wake of what happened. He seems like a guy that just lost his wife, is still trying to figure out how to cope with that."

He pauses, then adds, "That being said, I don't buy that shit about his hands and face for a second."

By and large, Marsh concurs with the assessment. He met Clady right after his wife was shot, and again the next day. Each time, he carried himself with the mix of anger and arrogance most Navy guys seem to possess. Besides that, there is no denying the other strong emotional presence Tinley referred to, the man clearly in a bad state in the wake of tragedy.

And just like his partner, he doesn't believe in the slightest that his newfound wounds have anything to do with an inability to sleep or some time spent on base in the evenings. What they do point to, he can't yet ascertain.

"Right," Marsh agrees, playing it through his head once more before lifting his gaze to Tinley. "So what next?"

He already knows what is next, and likely the move or two after that, but after scolding his partner earlier, he needs to throw him a softball.

Tear him down to build him back up, or some such cliché.

"Head out and knock on Mike Lincoln's door?"

Not a bad call, but considering what they have, there is a much more efficient way to handle things.

"Close," Marsh replies. "Since we have a photo ID and a witness confirmation, I called and requested a full search warrant. Judge Nagatsuka granted it a little bit ago. Should be here any minute."

Chapter Thirteen

A͏FTER SPENDING MORE than a decade in the SEALS, I've been privy to pretty much every form of training available. Weapons, physical combat, medical, even some comms work. In the elements, there aren't a lot of people better with maximizing whatever the environment has made available.

On the other end of that spectrum is my experience with modern technology, my cellphone about the most sophisticated piece of civilian equipment I've used with any amount of regularity. Trying to work an iPad inevitably ended with me handing it back to Mira or asking her a dozen questions along the way. My time on Facebook lasted about a week. Twitter was never even considered.

Just not my thing.

Even at that, it takes me less than twenty minutes of digging around on the internet to find what I am looking for. Armed with Mike Lincoln's name and a rough understanding of where he lives, what he does, and who he rides with, it doesn't take much more than a half-dozen websites to come up with an address.

Logging out of the online session, I watch as any history of my browsing is erased forever, grunting in satisfaction as a plain blue screen appears before me. Rising from my seat, I turn and head back in the same direction I just came from, nothing more than a couple of glances following me as I go.

Heading for my car, I slide out my cellphone and thumb down through my address book, finding the name I am looking for and hitting send. Sliding into the front seat, I turn the engine on and set the air conditioner to low, not bothering to pull out just yet.

On the third ring, the call is answered.

"Yo," Wendell Ross says.

Right now, Swinger and Stapleton are both at work on base. Either one would drop everything and come if I asked, just as they have so many times already, but after keeping them up all night, I wouldn't dream of bringing them in again.

Besides, the agreement was that I would make sure someone was in the loop at all times. Ross might not have been there when it was made, but his inclusion is more of an unspoken understanding.

"Hey, what's your schedule today?" I ask.

"I'm with the babies now while Bree is out running errands, but I can call her back."

"No," I reply. Looking to the rearview, I can see myself shake my head to either side. I can also see the heavy bags hanging under my eyes and the couple of days of growth sprouting from my cheeks.

Less than a week, and already I look like a man that's suddenly been cut free of the Navy and married life. Untethered.

Lord only knows what someone like Marsh must think when he looks at me.

"Nothing that pressing. How long will Bree be out?"

"Maybe a couple of hours," he replies. "What's up? Everything okay?"

I consider filling him in about the night before, but opt against it. If he hasn't already heard from Swinger or Stapleton, it can wait until I see him.

"Couple of hours is perfect," I say. "I have a few stops I need to make first. Swing by your place around three?"

"I'll be here," Ross replies. He doesn't bother asking his question directly again, this time opting to come in from the side. "Anything I need to have ready?"

"Just you," I reply, shaking my head again. "I'll stop in and say hello to everybody, then was hoping we could take a little drive."

To that, Ross doesn't say a word. He knows me well enough to know that I will get to it, will make sure he is provided with all the information he needs well beforehand.

I didn't bother writing down Lincoln's address before I left. It is committed to memory, and I wasn't about to put anything on paper that might be found later. Not with Marsh and his partner still lurking in the background, with the Wolves no doubt around and looking as well.

And it's not like there's a chance in hell of me ever forgetting it.

"I have an address for Mike Lincoln," I say. "I want to swing by this afternoon, see if anything jumps out."

"Okay," Ross replies, not a moment's hesitation. "Who's Mike Lincoln?"

"He's the guy."

It takes a split-second for this to register, for Ross to decode what I am telling him. "Oh. You mean..."

"Yeah," I say, again glancing to the rearview mirror, noticing the hardened stare that has settled over my features, "I mean."

Chapter Fourteen

BETWEEN GROWING UP IN NEBRASKA, going to college in Oregon, playing minor league baseball in Massachusetts, and now living in California, I have seen pretty much every corner of the country. With that, I have encountered every major fast food chain, every regional preference for architecture, even heard all the ridiculous speech patterns that exist.

And I have visited health care facilities the country over, developing a pretty standard understanding of what is to be expected.

Out front, there is patient parking. On the door is a sign welcoming guests and announcing hours. There are lots of windows and light and a vibe that generally seems inviting.

At the very least, there is something to indicate that the place is what it claims to be.

The address that Valerie Ogo gave me for Dr. Brendan Hoke has none of those things. From where I am parked along the curb, the place looks like nothing more than a standard home. Located in National City, it is two stories tall, a series of dinghy columns in dire need of paint lining the front. An oak tree and a pair of palm trees shade most of the front yard, keeping the sun from getting through, from grass being able to grow.

A chain link fence lines the front, a gate in the middle opening onto a concrete path that goes straight to the door.

If pressed, I would say the place looks like any of a number of houses along the street the Ogo's lived on, the structure as non-descript as a thousand others in the San Diego area. Twice I check the address she gave me, running the handwritten note against the map feature on my phone.

Both times it comes back telling me I am in the right place.

Exhaling slightly, I step out of the car and circle around the front. Across the street, a pair of elderly men in short-sleeve shirts buttoned to the throat both stare at me from their front porch. What's left of their hair is white, wary looks on their faces as they watch me go, neither making any effort to return the wave I give them.

Which isn't terribly surprising. The racial profile in National City is known to tilt heavily toward minorities. Considering where I am parked and the home I am walking toward, I can only imagine who they must think I am or what I am after, the make and model of my car not doing a great deal to assuage their concerns.

Lowering my hand to my side, I hurry up onto the sidewalk and through the front gate. In the distance, I can hear children at play, their preferred tone of speech just south of a shriek. A dog barks nearby as well, no doubt responding to the kids, telling them they are being entirely too loud.

In short, a snapshot of neighborhood life most anywhere in the country. An image that we ourselves were just getting accustomed to being a part of.

An eventuality I will only again experience in moments like this, snippets stolen while passing through, an outsider looking in.

Without my wife, there just won't be much point otherwise. I will forever be nothing more than an interloper, someone trying to peek over a fence for the sole purpose of seeing what lay beyond.

The faint hum of voices can be heard as I step to the front door and knock. The sound of it no more than falls away before the door is jerked back a couple of inches, a face appearing even with my chest.

A female somewhere around fifty, she presses either cheek tight between the door and the frame, her eyes narrow. "We don't want any."

"Any what?" I ask, my brows rising in surprise.

"Any anything," the woman replies. "We don't need insurance or candy bars and we already found Jesus."

For a moment, I have no idea how to respond. My brows track higher as the corners of my mouth rise just slightly, computing what this woman just said to me.

If pulling up in front of this place was a far cry from what I expected, her greeting was even further.

I consider asking her if she sees any candy or Bibles in my hands, if I really look like someone that would be out hawking insurance, but I decide against it. Already the woman is on the defensive, showing me nothing more than her face, making it clear that my presence is neither expected nor wanted.

"Is this the practice of Dr.-"

"Shh!" the woman snaps, bringing a finger up to her lips. "Do not say his name out loud." Again, she peers out in either direction. "How did you get this address?"

Confusion colors my features, a crease forming between my brows as I try to make sense of what I'm seeing. "Valerie Ogo gave it to me. She's the granddaughter-"

"Yes, I know who she is," the woman snaps, again cutting me off. Pushing the door open another couple of inches, she steps back and hisses, "Get inside. And hurry up."

Chapter Fifteen

THE NAME BRENDAN HOKE is clearly meant as misdirection. To hear it, one immediately thinks of a heavyset middle-aged white guy in chinos and a button down. Curly hair standing in a short halo around his head. Maybe a five o'clock shadow. Perhaps even throws a bit of Yiddish in to emphasis certain points.

Relies a bit on stereotypes maybe, but it's not like people don't immediately have preconceived notions when they hear I'm from the plains, or played baseball in college, or am a Navy SEAL.

They do often exist for a reason.

The man I'm standing in front of serves as the exception to every one of those reasons. The only thing about the man that is Caucasian is his name, his thinning hair white combed to the side, his skin three shades darker than my wife or her family. Wearing a thin moustache, he speaks with heavily accented English. What most people would misidentify as Indian, I recognize almost immediately as Pakistani.

Unintentional training provided courtesy of the United States military.

Extending a hand my way, he pumps twice, his grip soft, his skin damp, before releasing. "Mr. Clady, it is so nice to meet. Please, follow me."

He doesn't bother introducing himself, bypassing giving me the fake name or providing a new one. Turning back into the belly of the house, he leads me away from the living room and the impromptu waiting area it houses, a small handful of curious stares following me as we go.

The place is designed exactly as the outside would intimate. At one point in time, it was most likely a single- family dwelling, cheap wallpaper on the walls and linoleum on the floors lending themselves to such a supposition.

When that was, though, would be hard to say, the entire place renovated into a working medical clinic.

Pushing straight down the hallway bisecting the first floor, Hoke drops a hand atop the banister at the base of the staircase rising beside us. Using it as a pivot, he spins back toward the front, ascending the steps quickly, not once looking back to ensure I'm following him.

Not that he needs to, the handfuls of people filling what was once the dining room and a bedroom on the first floor doing it for him. In each space I catch glimpses of nurses and patients, all with various shades of skin tone, all openly staring at me.

On their faces are looks that range from curiosity to contempt, all seeming to wonder who gave the secret handshake to an outsider.

Following Hoke's movements, I spin around the base of the stairs and take them two at a time, rising through the center of the house. Eight strides later, I arrive on the second floor to find it ten degrees warmer, the air musty and dry. Dust motes float through stray shafts of light, illuminating an open floor plan free of walls or partitions.

Most of the area is used as storage, supplies of various sizes and shapes arranged along two of the walls. On the outside of their boxes, descriptions are stamped in a variety of languages, as are their expiration dates.

From what I can see, nothing they are using has been deemed safe for patient care in at least six months.

The third wall in the room is set up with an enormous bulletin board. Stretched from floor to ceiling, hundreds of pieces of paper are tacked up on it, all thrown together in a haphazard tangle. Seeming to lack any sort of cohesive system, they swirl in a random pattern, the sort of thing that would make sense only to the person that put it together.

Not that I don't have a sharp urge to go over and look, to scour it in hopes of finding my wife's name on there, seeing how this place fit with her passing.

The final quadrant of the room has been formatted as a makeshift office, a scratched wooden desk sitting along the wall with a mismatched chair on either side of it. A desktop computer that looks older than the model my mother and I had years ago is atop it, piles of files stacked to either side.

Again, the thought I had upon first arriving comes to mind, the place quite a way from any of the health facilities I've visited throughout the country.

In truth, it seems to coincide more with some of the places I saw in Guam and the Philippines.

Oblivious to my staring, Hoke walks straight to his desk and collapses back into the seat on the far side of it. The item moans under his weight as he lets his arms drape to either side before raising his hands to his face and rubbing vigorously.

Without being asked, I ease into the chair across from him, the seat every bit as stiff and uncomfortable as it appeared upon arrival.

"Please, forgive the greeting you received downstairs," Hoke says. "Most of our patients are informed to always come in through the alley and use the backdoor."

Taking it that I committed a bit of a faux pas, I dip my head and reply, "Apologies, I wasn't informed. I'll be sure to do that from now on."

If this conversation goes as I hope it might, there will be no next visit, no need for us to ever speak again, though I don't point that out.

Something tells me he doesn't need to hear it, anyway.

Waving a hand, he props his elbows on the arms of his chair and drops his hands into his lap. "Valerie Ogo called me earlier and said you would be stopping by. How can I help you?"

The crowd downstairs and the exhaustion on his features tell me he is the definition of the harried physician, with far more patients than time.

"Thank you for meeting with me. I know this was short notice, and I promise to be as quick as possible."

Once more, he waves a hand at me, dismissing the comment. What he means in doing so, I'm not sure, and not overly keen on finding out right now.

We both have more important things to get to.

"My name is Kyle Clady. My wife was Mira Clady."

I pause there, looking to get a sense of his reaction, to determine if it is overwhelming shock or exaggerated sorrow.

To my surprise, it is neither, at most a hint of confusion coming to his face.

"Clady," he says, repeating the name twice more. "It sounds vaguely familiar, but I can't place it right off. Is she a patient here?"

"No," I reply. "She was a social worker helping with Fran Ogo."

The mention of Ogo seems to be the words he needed, his face alighting with recognition. Sliding his hands up onto the arms of the chair, he adjusts himself in his seat, sitting up higher.

"Oh, yes! Yes, yes, yes. She was the woman that we were supposed to meet with on Friday, but unfortunately, she never showed." Stopping himself, as if realizing the next step in the sequence just as the words left his mouth, he looks up at me. "I hope everything is okay?"

It's not. In fact, nothing is okay. Has not been since last Thursday night and never will be again.

"No," I whisper, shaking my head slightly. "She passed away late Thursday night."

His eyes grow wider, a bit of color draining from his features. His mouth sags slightly for an instant, searching for the correct words, before he manages, "I am truly, very sorry."

I can tell the man's sentiments are sincere, but I need to keep pressing. I need to throw things at him quick and hard, keeping him off-balance, making sure the information I receive is unfiltered and true, that he has no chance to formulate any sort of narrative in his head, whether it be to protect him or me.

"She was shot," I say, watching as more color drains from his face, "by the same people that attempted to do the same to Fran Ogo last night."

By the time I am done, Hoke has leaned forward onto the front edge of his seat. Beads of sweat underscore the thin shafts of white hair that lay across his forehead. His mouth and eyes all seem twice their usual size.

"I...I..." he stammers. He looks around the room, eyes wild, trying to piece together what he's just been hit with.

Watching him, I can't help but feel bad about what I've done, of the way I've almost assaulted this man with the information, though there is nothing I can do about it. I meant no malice in doing so, merely putting together the best way I knew how to get the information I needed.

If it's any consolation to him, I can guarantee it all hit me infinitely harder a week before.

"Is Fran okay?" he finally manages to get out, swinging his attention my way.

"She is," I reply, "but only barely."

The look on his face tells me there is more he wants to ask, follow-ups dying to be lobbed my way, though I have no interest in letting those get out. I feel for the man and what he must be thinking, but he'll have time after I go to sort through things.

For now, I need to be as efficient as possible before being on my way again.

"The reason I am here now is that the two had never met before a couple of weeks ago, and that was only after Fran Ogo paid a visit to this office," I say. "The very same office they were all scheduled to return to less than eighteen hours after my wife was murdered."

The full range of human emotion seems to pass over Hoke's features as he stares at me. Beginning with sympathy, he cycles through shock and eventually horror before managing to stifle some tiny bit of it. Drawing in a pair of deep breaths, he again slides himself back in his seat before fixing his gaze on me.

"Mr. Clady, are you familiar with the Compacts of Free Association? Sometimes referred to as COFA?"

A day before, the question would have surprised me, but after speaking with the Ogo's already, I am ready for it.

Chapter Sixteen

As a rule, Elsa Teller never puts any names in her telephone. It is a small step to protect her contacts, a much bigger one to cover her own ass should anybody she doesn't want finding out who she's talking to comes snooping around.

Instead, she uses pictures. Not of the person in question – that would be equally foolish – but of small things that would instantly remind her of who it would be.

For Ringer, that image is the front tire of a motorcycle. For Myles Morgan, a pitchfork.

The image that pops up on her screen this time is a small shih tzu puppy. Charcoal gray, just a few stray white hairs frame its mouth and eyes, head tilted to the side, staring into the camera.

Despite the sound being turned off, the instant it shows up on the screen, the flash of color draws Teller's attention down. A single eyebrow rises slightly, staring at the image, knowing at a glance who it is. A tinge of surprise passes through her, fading quickly with the realization there is no chance she isn't taking this call.

"Excuse me, gentlemen," she says, rising from her seat and snatching the phone off the table before her, "I really must take this."

Seated at the small circular table with her are three men, all in sharp suits, all at least a decade older than her. Each pauses to watch her go, looks bordering on incredulous etched into their features.

As if they are the only damn clients she has.

Or are anywhere near the most important, now or ever.

Turning without another word, Teller exits the office and steps out into the hallway. Accepting the call, she marches past the receptionist's desk and through the front lobby, waiting until she is out on the sidewalk before pressing the phone to her ear.

"Teller."

"Hello, Miss Elsa," the familiar voice she had met with just that morning opens, "this is-"

"I know who it is," Teller says, the words coming out a bit harsher than intended but having the desired effect all the same. Just like no names appear in the phone, as few as possible are exchanged over the phone.

One would be amazed at the listening capabilities in the world today.

"How are you?" Teller asks, a tiny move to smooth over the prior comment, not caring in the slightest about the answer.

"I'm sorry to call so soon," Carmella Benitez says, "but I wanted to let you know about that thing you asked on this morning."

It takes no more than a fraction of a second for Teller to register what she is referring to. Taking another step from the door, she glances over a shoulder, making sure none of the men have dared to follow her outside, before saying only, "Ogo."

"Yes, her," Carmella replies.

"She came by?" Teller asks. Her voice inflection remains completely neutral as she asks. Having done this job as long as she has, she knows better than to ever get too hopeful, the number of possible pitfalls between a first sighting and final capture too many to count.

"No," Carmella replies, "but somebody else did asking about her."

Out of pure reflex, Teller again turns and looks over a shoulder. Seeing she is the sole person outside the building, she keeps her shoulders square, careful not to appear too cautious to anybody that might be watching.

"Who?"

"I don't know," Carmella replies. "Bigger guy, white, fit. He came to the front door – which nobody does – so I don't think he'd been here before."

Even without the description, Teller already had a pretty good idea of who it was. The physical dimensions only confirm it.

"What did he ask about?"

"I don't know," Carmella replies. "He waited a couple minutes, then Dr. Hoke came and got him, took him upstairs."

Falling silent for a moment, Teller considers the information. It isn't terribly surprising, though it does confirm that while Clady eliminated Lincoln, he doesn't seem content to stop there.

A problem that is likely going to end with more people being killed.

"Where is he now?" Teller asks.

"He left just a few minutes ago," Benitez replies. "I was with a patient, stepped out back as soon as I could."

Chapter Seventeen

THE PLACE LOOKS like a shit box, even by San Diego standards. The sort of the place where a person pays in cash on a month-to-month basis, brings in a handful of personal possessions, leaves shortly after arriving, a mountain of garbage in their wake.

A single story tall, the exterior had been painted tan an indeterminate number of years before. Not bothering to outline the trim or windows in a different shade, the entire place is the color of sand, a monochromatic scheme that blends perfectly with the front yard and driveway of little more than dirt packed tight.

Blinds shut tight cover all the windows. No cars sit in the driveway. Not even a single tire track denoting anyone has been by recently.

Standing outside the front door, Detective Malcolm Marsh inventories all of this in short order. None of it really surprises him, matching exactly with what he would expect from someone like Lincoln.

And perfectly fitting with everything about the Clady case thus far, not one aspect of it coming easily, for a variety of reasons.

"What do you think?" Tinley asks, the echo of his second round of knocking having faded away. In response, not a single sound has emanated from the house, the place as lifeless as the exterior denotes.

Giving the place once last glance, Marsh shifts his focus to the front door. He raises his voice and calls, "Mr. Lincoln, we have a warrant to search the premises. If you don't open up, we will be forced to enter."

Remaining where he stands, he waits thirty seconds for any form of a response.

When one finally does arrive, though, it isn't from within the house.

"I don't think he lives here anymore," a voice says, drawing the attention of both detectives toward the curb. Standing there is a woman that looks to be every bit of seventy, her short stature stooped forward, shoulders pinched inward. On her head is a hat with a brim as wide as her shoulders, obscuring all but the bottom half of her face.

Wearing a matching pink jogging set, she has a leash in her hand, a chihuahua at least as old as she is sitting on the ground by her feet.

"Haven't seen him in about a week."

Leaving Tinley by the door, Marsh steps down off the concrete block serving as a front porch. The sunbaked dirt of the front lawn feels like concrete beneath his feet as he closes the gap between them. Reaching to his hip, he extracts his shield, holding it up for her to see.

"Good afternoon, ma'am. My name is Detective Malcolm Marsh." He gestures with the badge over his shoulder, adding, "My partner, Detective Mark Tinley. Do you know Mike Lincoln? We were hoping to speak to him about an incident that took place last weekend."

The details he leaves purposefully vague, not wanting the woman to begin asking questions, about the case or Lincoln in general. More than once, Marsh has found that while neighbors – especially aging ones – can be good for noticing helpful tidbits, their curiosity can become equally burdensome.

"No," the woman says, "didn't even know Mike Lincoln was his name."

"But you know he hasn't been here?" Marsh asks, his brows coming together slightly.

"Oh, sure," the woman replies, "we all do. Been a nice break too, if you ask me."

Glancing back over his shoulder, Marsh makes no effort to hide his continued confusion. He takes another step forward, closing the gap between them, and asks, "How do you mean?"

Using her free hand, the woman motions to the garage door standing closed on one end of the home. "Well, I mean all those darn motorcycles. So loud, coming and going at all hours. Drives poor Kiki here crazy."

At the sound of its name, the dog looks up to the woman, blinking twice before lying flat on the sidewalk, already losing interest in the conversation.

"All those motorcycles?" Marsh asks, seizing on the first half of the woman's statement.

"Bunches of them," the woman replies, "four, five, six at a time. Great big guys, all on motorcycles, wearing leather vests. You'd think they'd get cold like that all the time, but they never seem to."

There had been no mention in Lincoln's file of him being affiliated with a motorcycle gang of any sort, though that didn't necessarily mean anything. Some guys took pride in sporting their colors at all times, while others made sure to shed them if they were being pinched by the police, a means of protection for other members of the outfit.

"What about Lincoln himself?" Marsh asks. "Did he wear a vest too?"

Scrunching her face slightly, the woman tilted the top of her head an inch to the side. "Sometimes, but not always."

Casting a quick glance to his partner, Marsh can see the young man is still rooted on the front porch, careful not to disrupt the balance of the impromptu interview taking place on the sidewalk.

Shifting back, Marsh considers what he's just found out, how it might fit into things moving forward.

In no way can he imagine Mira Clady or her husband being involved with a motorcycle gang in any way. What reason one of their members might have for shooting her in cold blood, or for even being in Balboa Park, is a mystery for the time being.

"When was the last time you saw him?" Marsh asks.

"Saw him?" the woman replies. "Oh, wow, maybe a month ago?"

Recalling what she had said just a moment before, Marsh circles back, silently cursing himself for the oversight. "How about hearing him? When was the last time his motorcycle was at home?"

"Today is, what, Wednesday?" she replies. "So maybe, last Friday?"

Chapter Eighteen

I HAVE one more stop to make before heading over to pick up Ross. As much as getting out to Lincoln's sits in the front of my mind, swirling with everything I just learned from Dr. Hoke, I can't push this part aside. I cannot let my overwhelming desire to figure out what happened to my Mira cloud the fact that I have other responsibilities as well.

Including looking out for what little family I have remaining.

The day has turned into standard spring fare in San Diego, the sun bright, the sky a cloudless blue. Despite the harsh glare thrown across my windshield, the air is actually not as warm as it appears, settling in the upper sixties.

Around me, the traffic is still somewhat thin, the afternoon rush still an hour or so into the future. Because of that, I would like to get through this stop as quickly as possible, but there is no way to rush things. Not with what I know now, with everything that still lies on the horizon.

The drive from Dr. Hoke's in National City up to the Paradise Valley Hospital is no more than a few miles. Dropping on and off the freeway, I make it in less than ten minutes. Little of it even registers with me, my mind still back in the house doubling as a medical clinic, chewing through everything that was just shared.

Which wasn't a huge amount of information, but it was a start.

Bypassing the parking garage on the edge of the grounds, I slide into a one-hour visitor stall closer to the front and kill the engine. Stepping out, I move in a quickened stride across the driveway separating the lot from the building, ignoring any painted crosswalks and heading straight for the front door.

Ditto for the front desk as I step inside. Averting my gaze to keep the overly perky orderly sitting behind it from even trying to offer assistance, I hook a quick right, operating on muscle memory, walking the same halls I had been in just eight hours earlier.

Underfoot, my sneakers squeak out an even rhythm against the buffed tile floors, the sound keeping pace with the thinking in my head, trying to put things into a coherent order. Locked in such a place, I don't hear Angelique if she tries to call my name. I don't even register her presence until I feel her hand on my elbow, thumb and forefinger locked around my ulnar bone. Pinching slightly, it is enough to jerk me back into the moment, my head snapping to the side.

"Hey there," she says. Releasing my elbow, she returns her hand to the cup of coffee clasped in the opposite one, both hands seeming to try and draw warmth from the steaming beverage.

In the time since I left, it doesn't appear that she has gotten a minute's rest. Still dressed in the same outfit, circles underscore each of her eyes, the skin of her face sagging just slightly.

Not that I can blame her. Losing one child and being called to the hospital for the other one is a hell of a stretch to endure.

Doing it without rest, doubly so.

"Hey," I reply. Walking parallel to her, I contemplate a hug for a moment, my hands rising a few inches from my sides, before thinking better of it. Laying one hand on her back instead, I ask, "How is he?"

Waiting until we make the corner, turning onto Hiram's hallway, Angelique nods slightly, "He still had a bit of arrhythmia this morning, so they want to keep him one more day. Doctor says it isn't that uncommon for someone that endured a major scare, especially one who, um..."

She glances down, not finishing the sentence. Not that she needs to.

Hiram is a big guy, someone that Mira used to affectionately refer to as *squishy*.

He knows it. There is no shame in admitting it, no point in pretending otherwise.

"Right," I say, saving her from having to make the statement.

Halfway down the hall, we come to a stop in front of the same trio of chairs we had first sat in fourteen hours earlier, alone in the middle of the night. Around us, the ward has come to life, daylight hours bringing out nurses and staff, physicians and family members, though still nobody seems to so much as glance our way.

Like the eye of a storm, we are a point of calm, everybody else swirling around us.

The irony of that, given all that has happened in the last week, isn't lost on me.

"But they still say he'll be just fine?" I ask.

Angelique lowers herself into the seat I used the night before. With the cup of coffee in her lap, her entire posture seems to lean inward, using it as a focal point. In such a position, she looks the smallest I have ever noticed, like the weight of things is finally getting to her, diminishing the woman before my eyes.

With the possible exception of my own mother, she is without question the strongest, most resolute woman I have ever known. Seeing how heavy things are beginning to sit on her only presses home just how bad they are, how much change has been wrought upon us.

Sliding into the seat next to her, I stare across the hall at Hiram's closed door. I focus on the plain blonde wood, pulling in air through my nose.

It's been five days since my Mira passed, and still I have no way of identifying what the triggers will be. When those moments will arrive that threaten to destroy the walls I have put up, letting the emotion I carry come spilling down.

Seeing her mother like this would crush Mira. Absolutely destroy her.

And the mere thought of that threatens to destroy me.

For a moment, the world goes blurry. Blinking fast, I can feel the moisture lining my eyelashes, my pulse throbbing through my temples.

"You okay?" Angelique whispers, having the grace not to look over, no doubt knowing full well exactly what I'm going through.

Not trusting myself to speak, I nod, waiting almost a full moment as it passes, tamped back into place. Raising my left hand to my face, I pinch my thumb and forefinger over my eyes before wiping the moisture across the leg of my jeans.

Only once I can trust my voice not to break do I say, "I just came from Dr. Hoke's."

"The one the Ogo's mentioned this morning," she replies, as if jogging her own memory of the prior discussion. "What did he have to say?"

Not sure where to begin, or how to best package things, I start simply with the first thing he said to me. "He didn't know Mira. Never even met her."

In my periphery, I see her face flash my way, her eyes wide. Holding the pose for an instant, she slowly turns back to face forward, saying nothing.

"But he knows the Ogo's," I continue, "namely, Fran."

Taking a breath, I pause as a pair of women walk past. Moving fast, they go in tandem, each clutching the hands of the other, neither saying a word.

"You heard mention of the word COFA this morning, right?" I ask, lowering my voice to almost a whisper.

Beside me, Angelique nods slightly, her chin rising no more than an inch.

"That's an acronym for the Compacts of Free Association," I say, "which is a kind of treaty that exists between the United States and the islands of Guam, Palau, and Micronesia. It's supposed to be an equal exchange agreement that lets the U.S. maintain military installations out there in the Pacific in exchange for giving their people access to free health and education services."

Prior to being stationed in Guam, I had never heard of such a thing. Kept well beneath the radar, it was the sort of thing the country entered into in case anybody came to wonder about their presence out there, but didn't really want broadcast to the masses.

Especially when it involved them actually having to make good.

"Or, as your daughter used to say, it was more of a flimsy apology for using their islands as target practice back when we were trying to develop nuclear bombs."

I can hear a small grunt beside me, a sound that is almost a snort, letting me know that Angelique is more than familiar with how the government handles such things.

As a first-generation immigrant, I have no doubt.

"As you can imagine, the fallout from all that testing rendered some of those islands uninhabitable, but there were other unintended consequences too. Radiation seeped into the oceans, affected sea life, was pushed into the airstream and breathed in. Nobody in the region was safe from it.

"Especially children."

Reciting the words almost verbatim from Dr. Hoke, I keep my gaze on the far wall. All thought of Mike Lincoln or going to pick up Ross have faded, now replaced by relaying the conversation from an hour before.

Which is as it should be. I'm not going through this alone. Others have the right to everything I know.

Not to mention, it's better for me to go slower, to take my time and ensure I don't do something foolish.

"When was this?" she asks.

"Back in the forties," I reply. "During World War II, right before we dropped them on Japan."

"So right about the time Fran was born," Angelique says.

One corner of my mouth ticks upward, a wan smile borne of appreciation and admiration. Even in the face of everything, she is able to immerse herself into the narrative, following my every word.

"She was two," I say. "And to jump ahead, she now has thyroid cancer and has come here to get the care that was promised her and many others under the Compact."

"And they don't want to provide it, which is why she went to go see..."

Again, she pulls up short of using her daughter's name, though that isn't the part I focus on right now. Instead, I winnow down to what she was saying, the conclusion she's drawn not entirely accurate, but pretty close.

"As you can imagine, there aren't a ton of COFA migrants coming into San Diego," I say, "at least not that many arriving in need of immediate health services. Most of those make it only as far as Hawaii."

I spare her the parts Dr. Hoke shared about the nightmare that is care out there, the state not having the providers or the funds to look after the scads of folks arriving regularly.

"Those that come here usually get shunted away from real facilities and end up in front of Dr. Hoke. A single man with a couple of nurses operating out of a house using supplies that fell off a truck years ago."

There is infinitely more I can share - even want to share. Thoughts the doctor had about the process, about the way people are handled, the manner in which they are funneled straight on past the system, the powers that be trusting that immigrant families will be devoured by the monolith that is American healthcare. About how many Fran Ogo's he has seen over the years, nothing more than a visit or two, enough to confirm a severe diagnosis, before they move on, never to be heard of again.

After a couple of minutes, Angelique lets out a garbled response. Sounding something like *damn government,* I nod emphatically in agreement, the things I've seen in my decade of service enough to make the common citizen sick with repulsion.

In truth, this is bad, but it isn't surprising.

And it damned sure doesn't even scratch the top ten of things I've borne direct witness to.

"How many like her does he think there are?" she eventually asks.

"No way of knowing for sure," I reply. "He said he's treated dozens over the years, but it isn't like there's a database out there."

"And he never met my daughter before?" she asks, the question and the underlying hints of disbelief both matching my response to the letter.

"You have to remember a few things," I reply. "First, there aren't that many of them. Most of who Mira worked with came in from the south, not from the west. Like I said, a lot of those stopped in Hawaii, made it to San Fran or Seattle if they were lucky."

Beside me, Angelique grunts softly, letting me continue.

"And those that do, most are older, don't speak English. It's not like they know a good attorney to call up or could pay for one even if they did.

"The doctor estimated of all the patients he's ever had, maybe two or three ever took it the extra step of getting an advocate on their behalf."

The familiar sounds of a working hospital fill the air between us, each of us processing, trying our best to superimpose the information we'd just gained onto what we already knew. Monitors beep, gurneys roll along, nurses talk to patients.

Throughout it all, we both sit in silence, trying to answer the same questions we've been chasing for the better part of a week.

Why her, and why now?

Chapter Nineteen

I WASN'T LOOKING for an exit strategy, perfectly content to sit in the hallway outside Hiram's room for as long as it took. For him to wake up, allowing me to go in and talk to him a few minutes. For my mother-in-law to work through everything I just shared, asking any remaining questions that linger. For me to make sure another moment like the one when we first sat down didn't surface again.

For five straight days, I have been surviving entirely on my SEAL training. Not so much the physical aspects, though those too have come to the fore, but the mental side of things. The parts that allow me to shove emotions into compartments. To narrow my focus down to a singular point, everything else just becoming extraneous noise.

Right now, that dot in front of me is finding out why my wife was murdered. Until then, I can't even think about her funeral, or my last days in the service, or what happens to the house, or going through the motions of everything required when a person passes away.

In the immediate aftermath of it, my attention was squared on finding her killer and making him pay. Once that was past though – and proved to only be a stepping stone along the path – it had shifted forward to where I am now.

If this is the end, I have no way of knowing. All I am certain of is I will follow it through for as long as it takes, wading through whatever the world puts in my way.

My Mira deserves at least as much.

Lost in such thoughts, I didn't recognize the sound of my phone buzzing. I didn't even it feel it in the front pocket of my jeans, vibrating against my thigh. Not until Angelique reach over, jabbing her forefinger just above my knee, did I even remember where I was and why I was there.

"Hm?" I asked, my eyebrows rising my forehead.

"You going to get that?" she asked, tilting her chin toward the outline of my phone pressed against the front leg of my jeans.

Pressing my back into the chair, I wrestled it free and held it before me, peering down at the screen.

"Valerie," I said. Looking to Angelique, I added, "I should-"

"Go," she confirmed, waving a hand, motioning for me to be on my way.

Accepting the call, I raised it to my face just long enough to say, "One minute," before lowering it back to my side. Aware of the rules on cellphone usage in hospitals, I kept it tucked by my side, glancing over a shoulder before turning my attention back to Angelique.

I myself could not care less if some nurse saw me and said something, but I wasn't about to bring anymore unneeded drama around my mother-in-law.

"Keep me posted. And please tell Hiram I stopped by."

"I will, and you do the same," she replied. Reaching out, she put a hand on my forearm, squeezing once before removing it, an unspoken blessing for me to depart.

Taking it as such, I shot straight up out of the chair, racewalking back over the route I'd taken forty minutes earlier. Weaving through the crowd of people filling the halls, I ducked outside to find the sun had already crested above me and was moving in the opposite direction, shadows lengthening across the ground.

Like just about everything since Mira was shot, time seems to have become a fluid concept, completely immaterial as it marches onward.

Now back outside of the hospital, I press the phone to my face. A bit of breeze picks up, blowing through the mouthpiece, as I say, "Valerie?"

"Yeah," she responds, "sorry if it was a bad time."

"Not at all," I reply, "I just stopped by Paradise Valley to check on Hiram. They tend to be pretty fickle about cellphones."

"Right," Valerie says, extending the word as if accompanied by a dawning. "How is he?"

Checking in either direction, I cross back over the driveway running alongside the hospital. Keeping my pace just shy of a jog, I use my key fob to unlock the doors and slide down into my car, leaving the door cracked beside me, replacing the warm air trapped inside with the cooler breeze blowing past.

"They're going to keep him one more night," I reply, "but he'll be just fine. How about you? Everything okay?"

A glance to the clock inset on the dash confirms what I was just thinking a moment before. Somehow, hours keep slipping by, already well into the afternoon.

For most of the day, the Ogo's were likely asleep. Now that they are awake, they no doubt are hungry and in need of some essentials, clothing and toiletries and such.

When I had promised as much to Valerie earlier, I hadn't yet spoken to the detectives. I didn't know the name of Mike Lincoln, certainly didn't know where he lived.

And I had gotten excited. I had gotten ahead of myself.

I had gotten sloppy.

"Yeah, we're okay," Valerie said. "I've been awake for a while, Nana just got up."

"I'm actually just wrapping up in here," I reply, "and then was going to head that way. I'm sure you're both getting hungry."

It's a lie, but for now the best I can do is hope she didn't notice. Considering the circumstances, I'm sure she'd do the same.

"We're actually okay," she says. "I walked down to the gas station on the corner while Nana slept and got us some stuff. We're all set on that front."

I've been at the Valley View long enough to know the closest gas station is a half-mile away, quite a hike to be making with an armload of groceries. Certainly further than *down on the corner.*

Still, I can appreciate the effort.

"But we need to go back to the house," she continues. "Nana is...she has medicines there. Things she needs that we didn't think to bring last night."

I catch the fact that she caught herself before telling me her Nana was sick. And that they never dreamed when we ran Hiram to the hospital that they would essentially be whisked away into hiding.

Going back to the house isn't really an option. Absolutely not for them. Not given how far out of town they are and the fact that there is definitely a few of the Wolves posted up nearby, scouting the place.

"I'm not far from there," I say, doing the math in my head. "Like I said, I'm over at Paradise Valley. What does she need and where is it in the house?"

I don't know how I'm going to get in and out undetected right now, but the logistics I'm not concerned with. I've made a career of carrying out operations a lot more complex.

Against enemies a lot more imposing.

For a moment, it seems like she is going to put up an argument, countering that they can't ask me to do such a thing, before she falls silent. Seeming to accept what I am saying, that it would be my final answer whether I was nearby or not, she exhales slowly.

"Okay," she replies, "but it's a long list. You're going to want to write all this down."

Chapter Twenty

Ringer is back in the corner booth where he feels comfortable. Where he doesn't have random strangers staring out through the front windows of In-N-Out at him. Where he doesn't have to put up with some overdone woman thinking she can call the shots.

Where he belongs.

Around him, his three deputies are grouped up, each looking exactly as they did the night before. Snapper, leaning back in his seat, engaged but wanting to put distance between himself and the disaster that happened at the Ogo's. Gamer, pissed at the world, sweating profusely.

Byrdie, the left side of his face resembling the aftermath of an allergic reaction, swollen twice the normal size. Staring straight into the center of the table, his one good eye is narrowed, his nostrils flaring.

In total, it is not a good look for the Wolves. A day ago, they were in control. They were grouped up in the bar, masters of their domain. They controlled the entire eastern edge of the city, nothing able to move without their say-so.

Now, one of their members was dead, another had been beaten badly, and they had been unable to secure a single octogenarian. Making things worse, they had no idea who was behind it, their only thread of a lead some snooty woman that walked right in on them, gun in hand.

Leaning forward in his seat, Ringer let all of this simmer. The bottom half of both arms splayed across the tabletop, he lets it all meld together, each aspect pushing the acrimony he feels higher. Every breath is louder than the one before.

This will never do. Not for him as leader, or for the organization as a whole. If things are left as they stand, if they don't act soon, word will get out.

And when it does, people a lot more imposing than one veteran and his fat sidekick are going to start gunning for them.

"Meeting was a waste of time," he opens. Low and measured, the words roll out in a grumble, drawing the attention of the others his way. "Woman had no idea who the guy is, says she'll get back to us."

Nobody says anything in response, seemingly waiting for him to continue. Having no more to add, he glances up to each of them in turn.

"That's it?" Snapper asks.

"That's all," Ringer replies. "She asked where Ogo is now, asked about the two men you guys saw, said she'd make some calls."

He doesn't add that the entire meeting took five minutes. That the drive there and back was almost ten times as long in total. That the damn line at the place was so long, he didn't even get a burger for his troubles.

"To who?" Snapper asks.

"Don't know, don't care," Ringer replies. "What I do know is, this shit has gone on long enough. Who do we have on the house now?"

Casting a glance between Byrdie and Gamer, Snapper looks his way. Seeming to be the unofficial spokesman for the group, he says, "Gold and Sprout."

To that, Ringer nods. Gold and Sprout both had more than a decade with the Wolves, had each been in more than their share of scraps. If there was any trouble, they would be up to the task.

Of course, not that long before he thought the same of Gamer and Byrdie.

"Any change?" Ringer asks.

"Nothing," Snapper replies. "They took over a couple of hours ago. Said nobody has come or gone from the place. Not even a sideways glance, like someone was scoping things out."

"How about them?" Ringer presses. A pair of grown men in vests sitting along a residential street isn't the easiest thing to hide. Keeping an eye on a house in broad daylight is almost asking for trouble, though right now that's a risk they have to accept.

Finding that woman, and by extension whoever has been messing with the Wolves, is of greater importance than any neighbors getting suspicious.

"Not that they mentioned," Snapper says. "Same for the morning crew."

Grunting softly, Ringer nods. He shoves himself back away from the table, running things in his mind.

Most likely, the Ogo's aren't going back to that house. His guys had one chance at it the night before, and through some combination of bad luck, timing, and sloppy execution, it had slipped by.

Now, they were left scrambling, hoping that somebody did something stupid or Teller got back to them with useful information.

Relying on others was not a situation he liked to be in. Nor did he feel the least bit comfortable with it.

"Linc?" he asks. He knows the answer to it already, but he has to follow up. Long past the point of any hope, he asks merely so his deputies hear it, nothing more than a box to be checked.

"Same," Snapper replies. "No change."

Which means the man's bike is still outside, his home untouched, his phone switched off. For a day or so, maybe that combination could occur. After a week, it's all but assured that he's gone.

And considering what happened the night before, it can't be considered a coincidence.

"Hey, Boss."

The sound is so unexpected, it takes a moment for Ringer to place it. He casts a glance around the table, already knowing the voice doesn't belong to any of his deputies, before sitting upright in his chair. Using his wrists as leverage, he cranes his neck upward, looking past Byrdie toward the bar.

"Yeah, Maxie?" he asks. Rarely does the man speak beyond asking their drink orders. Never does he interrupt.

For him to be doing so now means something is wrong, a bit of uneasiness settling into Ringer's chest.

"We've got company."

Chapter Twenty-One

MIKE LINCOLN WILL HAVE to wait for now. Or, at least, his house will.

The call from Valerie Ogo was a shift. It reminded me that there is more than just a single plotline evolving right now, that there is a lot more people than just myself involved in this.

No longer can I continue to be so selfish, so singularly focused as I move forward. Mike Lincoln is where all this started. He is the bastard that pulled the trigger, that ended the life of my Mira and irrevocably shifted the lives of so many others.

But he has been taken care of. He met his end less than a day after she did, in a way that could be construed as anything but humane. Whatever his house contains, whatever other secrets he has left to share, they will have to wait for now.

Sitting in the passenger seat of my sedan, I look over to see Wendell Ross behind the steering wheel. The same height as me, he is a few pounds lighter, his body the textbook definition of a SEAL. Dense, but not overly muscled. Capable of hand-to-hand fighting or long-distance running.

A fellow Petty Officer, he has been with us since the beginning of SEAL training as well. Like Swinger, he was a groomsman in my wedding. He was there with us at our favorite local bar the night of

Mira's death. He said goodbye to her for the final time not an hour before she perished, having no clue at the time how prescient the words would be.

He was also there with us the night we found Lincoln and took him out into the desert.

I have no qualms disclosing anything to the man, just as I know that Swinger and Stapleton would have no doubts about me bringing him along for this particular mission.

"So walk me through it again," he says, not bothering to glance my way as he maneuvers us through traffic. At this time of day, the freeway is heavy heading out of the city – and will be a bitch for us trying to get back later – but moving inbound it is fairly clear. Driving just north of sixty, we wrap in from his house in the suburbs, returning to National City for my third visit in the last twenty hours.

The directive doesn't clarify which *it* he means, though I can tell from the veins bulging along the back of his hands and forearms as he squeezes the wheel what he is referring to.

"Found the listing in her datebook at work," I say, stripping away all excess fat. "Gave a call, the woman that answered didn't speak a word of English, so I assumed that with her living in National City, she must be Hispanic. Called Hiram and together we rolled down for a visit."

Pausing there, I turn my head out the window, watching as exits for 28th and 30th pass by. I press my lips down tight, clenching my teeth for a moment, again feeling pangs of self-loathing for my own foolishness the night before.

The woman wasn't speaking Spanish. I should have recognized it right off. And even if I didn't, I never should have involved Hiram.

Angelique was right. He doesn't have the constitution that his sister had. He isn't made for this sort of thing.

"And?" Ross prompts, ripping me from my moment of self-flagellation.

"And when we get there, they invite us in for a second," I continue. "We have a conversation, doesn't last but a minute or two before I notice the doorknob turning."

I barely register as Ross pushes south, exiting from one freeway onto another, covering the last stretch of ground before National City, my mind back the night before. Visualizing the incident, I recall the glint of light off the polished knob that caught my eye.

"First one through was smaller, wiry," I say. "Middle-aged, maybe forty, packing. With civilians around, I had to neutralize the weapon, was able to gain the upper hand."

Flexing my right hand, I can still feel some tenderness in my knuckles, the swelling around the joints lingering. In turn, it triggers a ripple of pinpricks along the triceps of the same arm, the scab from the bullet that killed Mira grazing my arm finally beginning to heal.

"Second one through was built like a damn Dumpster. Sucker punched me upside the head, sent me reeling. Picked up his friend and bounced."

There is no obscuring the facts, not with Ross. We've been through enough together, I have no shame admitting I got my ass handed to me.

"By the time I picked myself up, they were running down the street, and Hiram was flat on his back having a panic attack."

That's as far as I go with the narrative. I don't fill him in about what happened to Hiram or the stitches now in my face. About Fran gathering the gun the Wolf left behind or taking them to a safehouse in the desert.

There will be time for all that soon enough. Right now, we just need to focus on this task. Getting in to the house, getting the medications that are needed, and getting back out.

Preferably without an end-of-workday public spectacle, but if it happens, so be it.

Receiving the information with little more than a series of nods and grunts, Ross processes it all. Like me and Swinger both in recent days, I can see our occupation rising to the surface, his concern for me as a human shoved aside, replaced by the machinations our training has instilled.

Strip away all but the most essential. Focus on how that applies to the end objective.

"So the house sits in the middle of the street," he begins.

"Yes," I reply, "though Valerie told me there is an alley that runs a block behind it. You can drop me off there and I'll go in on foot."

The corner of his mouth hooks downward, the tiny frown the closest he ever shows to disapproval.

"Where were they parked last night?"

"End of the street," I say. "North, near the intersection."

"Weapons?"

"Mark 23," I reply, the make and model one he knows intimately well, it being the gun of choice for SEALs.

This gets a tiny nod of approval before he falls silent again. A long-time resident of the city, he knows the area well enough to know where to drive without being instructed, his focus never leaving the road.

Exiting down off the freeway, we wait through a traffic light before heading south, falling into the gridded streets of local neighborhoods. Much more active than my previous visit, handfuls of cars slide past, people just returning home from work, anxious to get off their feet or get dinner on the table.

Nobody so much as glances our way, a minority behind the wheel no sort of abnormality in this part of town.

"No way they're not still on the house," Ross says. "I'll drop you in the alley, then circle around out front."

Considering it a moment, I counter, "They might know the car, though. I drove it here last night."

"That's the idea," he replies. "Hopefully, it'll get them to reveal themselves, maybe even buy you a couple of extra minutes."

I hadn't thought of that, though the reasoning makes sense. Even if they had a make and model on the car, that wouldn't trump the most basic of instructions, which would be to look for a thirty-something white guy. Once they saw it was Ross driving, they would be out of position, probably a little pissed, in no way paying attention to the house.

Raising a finger, I tap on the glass beside me.

"There's the alley. Turn here."

———

The interior of the airport was every bit as small as the name Eugene Airport would indicate. Not going the unnecessary step of assigning someone's name to the place, or doing as they had in Missoula and deeming it an international airport because it made the occasional hop into Canada, the place held no pretension about what it was.

A small, single terminal affair that hosted a small handful of arrivals and departures each day from an even smaller handful of airlines.

Replete with an off-brand book store and a small mini-mart, the place was free of pretension, a harsh contrast to Portland International, the only other option for making my way back to Corvallis.

Which, given my state, was kind of the point.

The harsh chill of December greeted me as I stepped off the small aircraft. It swirled the length of my body, icy crystals pelting my skin, as I clamped my jaw tight. Lowering my forehead into the breeze, my right hand held tight to the strap of my duffel bag, keeping the overstuffed item pressed tight to my knee.

My opposite hand was pinned tight against my chest, fingers curled into a ball to protect them from the cold air. Held in place by the omnipresent sling that had become the bane of my existence, I walked across the concrete expanse toward the terminal, moving in exaggerated strides.

Along either side, people moving much slower fell by the wayside, my singular focus on getting inside. On freeing myself from the cold air that enveloped me, causing every muscle to seize tight.

On seeing my Mira again.

Ignoring the urge to use the bathroom, the scratchy feeling in my throat from breathing plane air for the last couple of hours, I passed beneath the fans pushing out superheated breeze above the entrance into the terminal. As I burst through, I caught a few surprised glances from passengers already lining up for the next flight out, many dressed in shades of gray or brown, much better suited for the chill outside.

Not that I gave them more than a passing glance.

The last few months had been an exercise in masochism. Not only had the universe decided to take away the game I loved so much, but it had opted to do so in a way that ensured I couldn't be near the woman I loved either.

And serving as a double indignation, it had even gone the extra step of mandating I do so under a certain level of inertia.

None of which were things I was especially good at.

As I had been told an inordinate number of times, a torn rotator cuff was not especially rare. Especially not for a baseball player, it actually ranking as one of the more common injuries.

Pitchers that threw from awkward angles. Guys that slid headfirst and snagged something they shouldn't.

A person like me laying out for a catch and coming down on it wrong.

I also knew that a dislocated shoulder wasn't too terribly uncommon either. A simple ball-and-socket joint, there wasn't a tremendous amount of skeletal structure keeping it in place, most of the heavy lifting there done by soft tissue.

The problem, and what made my situation so rare, was that in only the most extreme of circumstances did both things happen simultaneously.

What that meant for the recovery time, or even my future in baseball, was not yet clear, questions that I had purposely pushed to the back of my mind. Instead, I had filled the necessary three-month waiting period by dutifully wearing the sling at all times, meticulously planning out my rehab schedule to fend of going stir crazy.

An approach that I would say worked for me with only nominal success.

Even less for my poor mama.

"Welcome to Eugene Airport..." an automated voice announced, pulling me from my thoughts. Increasing my pace slightly, I hefted the bag up a few inches, adjusting my grip as the sign for the exit appeared on the overhead signage.

Five months.

Five long months had passed since I'd last seen Mira. Never had either of us intended to let it go so long, the plan originally for me to have returned at the end of the season months before.

In the wake of the surgery, though, that had gotten pushed back. One time after another she had implored me to come out anyway, but there was no way I could impose in such a way on her. Not in that condition, virtually worthless for those first few weeks, relying on mama for every-thing as I slowly figured out how to live with one hand.

It had been hard. I had missed her fiercely every day, bombarding the poor girl with text messages and emails, if for nothing else than to just feel like I had someone to talk to, wiling away the hours each day.

And now, at long last, it had passed.

The reunion wasn't one from a movie, with two people calling out to one another amidst a busy big city airport. It didn't involve the two of us sprinting through a torrent of strangers, shoving people aside, focused on seeing each other.

It damned sure didn't have a cheesy background soundtrack.

What it did have was the most beautiful woman I had ever seen standing just outside the door separating the terminal from baggage claim, her dark eyes shining. It had a small handmade sign in her hands with my name written across, a playful gesture I couldn't help but laugh at the instant I saw it.

Just like it had the fiercest one-armed hug to ever occur, neither of us even minding the extra limb folded between us.

And it had the longest, deepest, most passionate kiss the Eugene Airport had ever witnessed.

It had everything I'd been missing so much, the look and touch and feel and smell of all I'd missed so much.

In short, it had my Mira.

Chapter Twenty-Two

THE KEY IS to look completely natural. To not be furtive, casting glances to either side, checking to see who might be watching. To not have a hand cocked by my hip like some Old West gunslinger, ready for a show-down in the streets.

To walk nice and slow, my pace never quicker than necessary, my arms and legs moving in a relaxed gait.

Climbing out of the car at the end of the alley, I start forward, the concrete path wide enough to provide ample space for a single lane of traffic, but definitely not enough for two cars to try and slide past one another. Lining both sides are the rear entrances to homes and small apartment complexes, fences separating them from the thruway. Some are wooden, slats standing taller than I am, making it impossible to see what's beyond. Others are chain link, providing glimpses into standard family dwellings, swing sets or clothes lines dotting the yards.

A few have dogs, or at least signage warning of them. Almost all have oversized plastic bins along the back, black for garbage, blue for recycling.

If the street I live on served as a basic snapshot of suburban life, this was a pretty accurate depiction of neighborhoods in an urban setting.

Starter homes for people like the Ogo's. A place where a family like Mira's lived before moving on to their new location.

Walking forward, I ease myself to the left side of the alley. As I move, I count the houses, trying to visualize the fronts of them, matching the color of their paint with the quick glimpse I got of the area the night before.

It proves a futile task, my few memories coming back in ragged snapshots, the combination of trying to help Hiram and taking a wicked shot to the cheek both making any level of detail almost impossible to recall.

Instead, I focus on the details that Valerie provided on the phone, walking by the better part of a dozen homes before finding what she referenced.

From the back, the home the Ogo's stay in is solid white, the owners having not made the time or financial investment to bother with paint. Strips of dirt and grime line the undersides of the aluminum siding that cover the backside, a few spots of rust forming around the corners of metal window sills.

None of those things are too distinctive, falling in line with the vast majority of homes I've already walked past. What confirms the place is the address I'm looking for is the aging washer and dryer parked beneath a lean-to. Sitting on the concrete walkway along the back of the home, they are covered by a small awning, the top nothing more than a piece of unfinished plywood.

Beside it is an older model woman's bicycle, the body painted mint green, with a banana seat and a basket on the front.

Any home can have dirt or rust, but only a very specific one would have both of those things sitting out in plain sight.

Careful not to break stride, I can feel my heart rate pick up just a tick as I cast a glance the length of the alleyway. Made for passage and not for parking, there are no cars visible, nowhere for them to hide even if they wanted to.

If the Wolves are nearby, they're out on the street.

Or maybe they took the extra step of going inside. Perhaps after we left for the hospital last night, they circled back, deciding to wait for somebody to return.

The odds of that are low, the chances that they are still here almost a day later even lower, but I can't go in making assumptions. That's how mistakes are made. How people get hurt or worse.

The gate on the rear of the property is exactly like the front, nothing more than a simple latch. Raising it upward, I swing it open just enough to pass through before closing it in my wake. Careful to make as little noise as possible, I pass straight over the patchy grass of the backyard, puffs of dust rising around my feet with each step.

As I move, I check each of the rear windows in order.

There are four in total, three on the first floor, just a single one extended out from a dormer on the second. Two of the four have lace curtains pulled closed over them, the thin material hanging lank, not giving away any signs of movement.

The other two are open, one positioned where I would expect it to look out from above the kitchen sink, the other from the upstairs window. Each with the sun reflecting off them, I can't make out anything behind them.

The fingers on my right hand flex just slightly, practically itching to reach for the Mark 23 tucked above my haunch, though I refrain from going for it just yet. I'm still too exposed at the moment, the yard visible to at least a handful of houses on both sides of the alley. Needing nothing more than a single bored or nosy neighbor to be staring out the window, I keep the weapon stowed.

The key to the backdoor is tucked up under the top corner of the awning extended over the laundry machines. Pausing just long enough to slide the pads of my fingers against the rough wood, I find the brass implement and pull it down, barely breaking stride as I unlock the door and step inside.

The instant I am in, the rear entry shut behind me, I jerk my gun free. The textured grip fits snug in my hand as I extend it straight before me, left hand cupped beneath it for support. Swinging it from left to right, I make one quick pass over the space, seeing nothing, before bringing it back slow in the opposite direction.

My breathing evens out, my senses turning to steel, years of training taking over I assess the situation before me.

The home looks exactly as it did eighteen hours earlier, from the shattered coffee table in the center of the room to the drywall dust on the floor from the few errant shots the Wolf managed to get off in our tussle.

Best I can tell, nobody else has been through, not a stray footprint or out of place shard of wood to signal any trespassing.

Though that doesn't mean they haven't been through.

Sweat comes to my face, the warm air of the house raising my body temperature, as I scan for any sign of life.

Best I can tell, the sole movement in the place are the dust motes floating lazily through the light streaming in through the rear windows.

Chapter Twenty-Three

THE BAR IS KNOWN as The Wolf Den, a not-so-clever moniker given to it no doubt by the motorcycle gang of the same name that calls it home. Made almost entirely of wood, the place looks like it was thrown together decades before, now held together by little more than nails, fading paint, and termites holding hands.

The only signage of any kind is a wooden sign running along the top of the awning extended out over the porch, white lettering against a dark brown background. No logos or emblems of any kind. No mention of hours of operation anywhere.

Detective Malcolm Marsh has never been to the place, has never even heard of it, but he isn't surprised by what he sees. It's the sort of place he would expect someone like Mike Lincoln to frequent, the line of motorcycles parked out front hinting that he is far from the only one to consider the place a second home.

"Third bike in from the right is Lincoln's," Mike Tinley says from the passenger seat. Holding up a piece of paper with Lincoln's plate number scribbled on it, he alternates his glance between the sheet and the row of bikes parked across the street, checking once more, before dropping the paper back atop the stack of printouts in his lap.

The search of Lincoln's home turned up precious little, the place a complete dump that looked to have been abandoned days ago, if not before. Spending a total of only ten minutes inside, Marsh had cut the search short after realizing there was absolutely nothing to be gleaned from sifting through the wreckage of the man's life.

Fast food wrappers, sweat-stained sheets, and moldy dishes tend to not provide a lot of workable evidence.

Stepping outside before the stench of the place permanently seeped into his skin and clothes, Marsh left with just a single thing in his possession. Now tucked into the front console of their sedan, he glances over to the matchbook he'd snatched from the ground beside what Lincoln used as a bed, the words The Wolf Den spelled out in the same script as those above the front door.

"Should we call La Mesa PD and ask for backup?" Tinley asks, his voice already carrying the slightest tinge of anticipation.

Recognizing it instantly, Marsh cast a sideways glance to his partner, hopeful he isn't about to say or do something they could both come to regret.

"No," Marsh replies. "Odds are, he isn't here, and if we arrive with a force, it's only going to escalate things. Let's just go in, ask if they've seen him."

"But his bike is parked right there," Tinley replies, raising a finger and extending it toward the row of motorcycles parked along the front.

"Don't point," Marsh says, feeling his frustration with his young partner rise, "and don't call them bikes."

Without waiting for a response, Marsh steps out of the car. He checks either direction before stepping across the street, a thin plume of dust kicking up, blowing across his body as he walks.

A moment later, the sound of a car door slamming shut behind him can be heard, Tinley jogging to catch up with him. For perhaps the first time ever, the younger man has the good sense to remain quiet, the two ascending the trio of steps together.

The front entrance has been formatted to mirror an Old West saloon, an actual door replaced by a pair of swinging gates. Careful to hide the eyeroll he feels at seeing them, Marsh pushes through, taking no more than a step inside before stopping.

An instant later, Tinley appears beside him.

Sliding his sunglasses down off his face, Marsh takes a moment, letting his eyes adjust to the darkened interior of the room. As he does so, he makes a quick scan, the place confirming what the outside hinted at, in lockstep with every preconceived notion he had before entering.

Nothing more than a single room, the place has one roughhewn bar along the wall and some remainder furniture spread throughout the rest of the room. On the walls are an odd assortment of neon beer signs and mounted animal carcasses.

None of them are wolves.

Despite the number of motorcycles parked out front, there is no more than a half-dozen people inside the place. All male, all white.

All looking directly at them.

"Help you with something, officers?" the man behind the bar asks. A thick older man with white hair and paunch, he stands leaning against the front of the bar, a towel over his shoulder.

Despite his genial expression and non-threatening tone, Marsh recognizes what the opening question was really meant to relay instantly.

They were pegged as law enforcement the moment they entered, if not before. They are not welcome, which is why the bartender is the one talking to them.

Reaching to his hip, Marsh forces a smile into place. He hates the awkward feeling of it, even more the fact that he has to ask nice, pretending to kiss these ignorant redneck's asses.

They are trained detectives. He has a law degree. His partner has a BA from San Diego State. And yet they have to play the part if they want any sort of cooperation.

Disgusting.

Extracting his shield, Marsh says, "Detectives, actually." He puts the badge away, motioning from himself to his partner. "Marsh and Tinley, SDPD."

The bartender says nothing, doesn't move an inch, merely staring back at them.

Taking a few steps toward the bar, Marsh says, "We need to speak to a Mike Lincoln. We understand he frequents this place."

The man's eyebrows rise, faux surprise coloring his features. "Frequents? I wouldn't go that far. He stops in from time to time, same as anybody else."

Flicking a glance to the corner, Marsh can see the quartet of men that had turned and openly stared upon their arrival have since shifted their focus. None are looking over, though they don't appear to be in conversation either, no doubt listening to every word being shared.

"When was the last time you'd say you saw him?" Marsh asks.

"Couldn't, really," the man says, playing the part of ignorant rube to perfection, "been a while, though. Maybe a couple of weeks?"

Marsh hasn't been inside this particular place before, but he's been inside enough like it to know how things work. Things are predicated on a hierarchy, a single person in charge, things filtering down in order from there.

Right now, the head guy is probably one of the two large guys in the corner, either with the long hair or the bald head. The others would be his deputies.

In no world does the bartender even make the list. He is so far down, he is essentially a dog, something that is seen but never speaks. The fact that this one is doing so now, without so much as consulting the others, tells Marsh that everything he is being told is bullshit.

Whether that's because they have something to hide or that is simply how they deal with law enforcement, he can't be certain.

"Weeks?" he asks. "But isn't that his Panhead parked outside?"

"I don't know," the guy says, "maybe. A lot of the guys leave their rides here sometimes. Certain neighborhoods have noise ordinances and such, so they park them here during the week."

The answer is just the sort of canned crap Marsh expects, close enough to reality to maybe be true, while more likely being a complete fabrication. Either way, it is fast becoming apparent that they won't be gaining anything useful from sticking around.

The only thing they've picked up for certain is that Lincoln isn't present, none of the men in the place even close to the picture from Balboa Park or the mugshot he has on file.

"What's this all about?" the barkeep asks, his brow coming together slightly. "Mike in trouble for something?"

Flicking his glance to the side again, Marsh can see just the tiniest move from one of the men. Coming from the man on the left edge, a tangle of teeth jutting out over his bottom lip, he leans a few inches to the side, as if trying to listen a little closer to whatever is being said.

"Oh, no, nothing like that," Marsh replies. "We just needed to get a witness statement from him about something is all. I'll be sure to stop by again in a day or two, try to catch him then."

Chapter Twenty-Four

THE HOUSE ISN'T NEARLY AS big on the inside as it appears from the outside. A simple one-bedroom affair, the entire first floor is nothing more than the room I had been in the night before. A large living room that feeds directly into an open dining room. Behind it is the kitchen, the only thing to offset it from the rest of the space being a metal strip on the floor separating hardwood from linoleum.

Upstairs is the single bedroom with a pair of beds, both twin sized, with a full bathroom carved out in the corner. Like my first impression of the place downstairs, everything looks to have been remainder from the seventies, as if the place was rented furnished from an older couple that had been there for most of their lives before being shunted off to a nursing community somewhere.

The walls on all four sides slope inward, accommodating the pitch of the roof. Light filters in through a single window in the bathroom and along the front wall. It is at least ten degrees hotter than the first floor, sweat dripping off my nose.

Painfully aware of each second that slips by, I stand in the tiny bathroom. A plastic sack in hand, the vanity mirror in front of me has been flung open, standing perpendicular to the wall. Behind it is row after row of medicine vials, most with names I don't recognize.

I have no doubt where many of them came from.

None of them have a prescription label, or even a patient name, on the side. All of them have been expired for at least a couple of months.

The gun is stowed back behind my hip as I work, the sack in one hand, my phone in the other. On the screen is a list of medicines needed for Fran, Valerie having sent it over a while before.

One at a time, I scroll down through, matching names and dropping them into the bag. Thus far, I have seven already accounted for, at least as many still remaining.

Flicking my gaze back and forth, I check the label on a bottle before me. Sliding back to compare it to the list, the screen dissolves, replaced by an alert letting me know I have an incoming call.

Wendell Ross.

Thumbing it on, I press it to my face, my pulse increasing just slightly. "Yo."

"Far side of the street," he says. "Two guys, both in their thirties, white. Small tan sedan. Couldn't get a plate."

My first impulse is to go to the front window and peek out, to see the bastards, or more importantly, let them see me.

Just as fast, it passes. This is no time for anger to cloud my judgment. Not with the medicine Fran needs in hand, certainly not with Ross out on the street to run interference.

Even if it does still piss me off.

"They make you?" I ask, realizing how foolish the question is even before I'm done asking it.

If it offends him in the slightest, he doesn't let it show.

"Negative," he replies. "We must have caught them at shift change. Street was clean on first sweep. Second pass turned up these two."

"They moving at all?"

"Negative," he repeats, "but their target is obvious."

He adds nothing to it, but he doesn't need to. Already I am aware that I have been inside for ten minutes, that every additional second I spend increases the chances of somebody seeing me or something bad happening.

"Two minutes," I say. "Opposite end."

"Roger that," he answers, not challenging me in the slightest on the timing or the location.

Cutting the call, I slide the phone back into my pocket. Giving up on the list, I grab everything I can see, snatching the vials up two and three at a time and depositing them in the sack.

They'll know what they need. Better to have too much than not enough.

Wiping the tray clean of everything, I close the mirror and give a quick scan of the bathroom. Standard tub, toilet, sink arrangement, nothing else visible beyond the cup with a pair of toothbrushes. Grabbing both, I deposit them into the sack, exiting back into the bedroom.

If I had more time, I would put together a go-bag for them. I would snatch up handfuls of clothes, anything else they might need.

But not now. Not with two men sitting on the curb, waiting for me to make a mistake. Not with a sack full of needed medicines and a handful of other places I still need to be getting to.

I don't bother extracting the Mark 23 as I ease my way down the stairs. Ross has already made the surveillance team, would have alerted me if there was any danger. Instead, I move as quickly as silence will allow, heading out the back door and locking it in my wake.

Every part of me would rather be going through the front. I would prefer to throw open the door and step onto the concrete landing, letting them see me plain. Slowly, I would turn and lock the door behind me before shifting and looking straight at them.

Maybe I would wave. Maybe I would wag my gun at them.

Maybe I would jog right over and do to them what I did to their cohort the night before, flailing away until whatever tensile strength remains in my right hand is shattered.

But I don't, for a variety of reasons. While doing all that might make me feel a little better, it would present a litany of problems. Onlookers. Law enforcement. Tipping off the Wolves.

Destroying my already aching hand.

Choosing to hang onto the key, I lock the rear door and walk across the backyard. Plastic sack in hand, I swing through the rear gate and exit in the opposite direction, never once moving too fast or appearing to be a in a hurry.

My face is sweaty and my senses are heightened, but to the average observer, nothing is out of the ordinary.

Chapter Twenty-Five

MYLES MORGAN CAN SMELL BLOOD. Like a shark attracted to chum in the water, he can pick up the scent of a single drop floating in an ocean. Entering through his nasal passages, it goes straight to his brain, processed and sent to every nerve ending in his body.

Bordering on euphoric, it is the reason he is in the position he is, has ascended as fast as he has.

Leaning forward, his elbows resting against the front edge of his desk, it is all he can do to keep the smile from his face. His tongue flicks out over his bottom lip, glancing between the two men across from him, their heightening discomfort only adding to the moment for him.

He has them. They know it. And now he knows it.

There is no better feeling. Not drink or smoke or even sex.

Power, raw and unbridled.

"So, gentlemen, do we have a deal?"

The pair glance between one another. Spitting images of each other thirty years apart, they are a father and son team, the sort of duo that thought they could get into this business and hang with the larger players in the market.

And now they were getting their asses handed to them as a result.

The question was phrased to make it appear like the men had a choice, but it was anything but. They were going to take pennies on the dollar for their tiny operation, and another annoying burr was going to be out of Morgan's hair, gone forever.

All they had to do was agree and sign.

"Well, we'd really like a bit more time to look this over," the younger of the two says. A snotty kid name Bret, he isn't a day over thirty, appearing as if he doesn't need to shave more than a time or two a week.

His very presence annoys Morgan.

"And people in Hell want ice water," Morgan replies, the comment drawing stares from both men across from him. "If you guys want to receive even a nickel for the time and energy you've spent building this thing, you'll sign right now."

The time for niceties is passed. He gave them a moment to save face, but it is gone. Now it is time for them to be on their way.

He has dinner plans to soon be getting to.

"I just think-" Bret begins, still trying to save face.

Morgan will have none of it.

"And I think it is time for the grown-ups in the room to do the talking." Shifting his focus to the elder of the two, he says, "Don't you, Brent?"

Across from him, the younger man looks incredulous, like he might again make the mistake of opening his mouth.

His father has no such problem, his face defeated, his features ashen as he stares down at the documents in his hand. He is going to sign. He sees there is no way around it.

Nothing can save him now.

The knock on the door is short and terse, just two quick taps, but it is so unexpected it might as well have been a percussion grenade. Snapping Morgan's attention away from the desk, his eyes blaze, ready to fire his secretary the instant this meeting is over.

Her rich city councilman uncle be damned.

"Mr. Morgan?" she says, sticking just her head in through the door, nothing visible save the chin up.

"What?" he replies, his gaze hard, the look alone letting her know she has messed up beyond repair.

For the first time, she seems to have received the unspoken message, her body language relaying she isn't completely oblivious. "Um, you have a visitor."

Nostrils flaring, Morgan glances to the men. Just two feet away, the older of the two still stares dejectedly at the pages in his hand, his son watching the back-and-forth with something bordering on amusement.

An expression that just cost them both another ten thousand dollars.

"*I'm in a meeting.*"

"I know, sir, but it's *her.*"

The next response was already lined up, resting on the tip of his tongue, ready to be fired off. With just one single word, she manages to shove it aside, saying the only thing in the world that could possibly justify her behavior.

Not that he's any happier about it.

"Gentlemen, excuse me a moment," Morgan says, standing and exiting the room without so much as a glance their way. Striding for the door, his secretary is gone by the time he gets there, completely out of sight as he steps into the reception area outside his office.

In her stead is a single person, someone Morgan could go a lifetime without ever seeing again.

"What do you want?" he snarls. "I'm in a very important meeting. I'm about to-"

"I don't care," Elsa Teller replies. Dressed in a sleeveless black dress and heels, she waves a hand at him, the French tips of her fingers flying by. "Whatever it is can wait."

A flush of heat rises to Morgan's cheeks. He can feel his face glow red, sweat threatening to ooze from his forehead and upper lip.

Nobody speaks to him that way, not even her. Especially outside his own office.

"Now you listen here-" he says, raising a finger before him.

"Clady found Hoke."

For the second time in as many minutes, Morgan is cut off mid-sentence, whatever he was about to say rendered moot. A puff of air passes over his lips as he stares at her, trying to compute what she is telling him.

"And you might want to put that away before you hurt yourself," she adds, glancing down to his finger still extended her way.

Ignoring the barb, Morgan slowly lowers his hand to his side. He draws in a pair of deep breaths, computing what she's just told him.

"He...how do you know?"

Raising her eyebrows slightly, Teller glances around the lobby. Nobody else appears to be nearby, not even the receptionist that seems to have apparated from the office.

"You really want to do this here?" she asks.

"I don't want to be doing this at all," Morgan snaps. His office is being used. Already he's excused himself, no way is he going to ask them to exit. "How credible is it?"

"Eyes on him sitting down with the doctor."

"In person?" Morgan asks, his eyes bulging slightly.

"Be kind of tough to sit down with someone otherwise, wouldn't it?" Teller counters.

Bitterness rises like bile along the back of Morgan's throat. If he could, he would cut ties with her in an instant. He would make sure she never worked on the west coast again, preferably anywhere in the country.

He'd ensure he never so much as heard a whisper of the name Elsa Teller again.

But the decision to go with her was made a long time before at the only level that was above his. Getting rid of her would have to do the same.

"I thought this was being taken care of?" Morgan asks.

"It was, but things have changed," Teller replies. "Turns out the guy is a bit smarter than we might have thought. Which is good for him, but bad for anybody else he might have talked to."

Leaning back, Morgan exhales slowly. He considers what she is saying, finally understanding why she has come to see him.

Her job has a fair bit of leeway in it, free range she has been extended for completing certain tasks, but she isn't at liberty to make all decisions on her own. The go-ahead for those must come from a ranking official within the organization.

Someone like him.

"How wide are we talking?" he asks.

"Enough to finish it," Teller replies.

"And you're certain they can get it done?"

The right corner of her mouth turns upward, a small smirk rocking her head back half an inch. "Considering everything that has happened in the last day or so? Yeah, I'm pretty damn sure."

Morgan has no idea exactly what she's referring to, and he doesn't want to. Already this has grown bigger than it should have, extending much further than any of the other ones.

"Just make it go away," he mutters.

Both eyebrows rise as she nods, a bit of surprise coloring her façade. "There could be some unforeseen costs associated with doing so."

"Just make it go away."

Chapter Twenty-Six

BOTH OF THE beds in the room beside mine have been made, each of the Ogo women awake and showered. On the round table in the corner sits a small assortment of items that Valerie had picked up from the gas station, chips and power bars and a handful of other snack items. I'm guessing drinks line the shelves of the minifridge in the corner, the appliance humming loudly, making sure we are all well aware of its presence.

Added to the collection are the pair of sacks I brought with me, one the medicines from the Ogo's home, the other more food from the Von's I passed on the way out here. Mostly deli items, it is filled with sandwiches and pasta salad and a few other odds and ends, light only the chicken tenders I ate in the car as I drove.

They were terrible, salty and overcooked, but they were protein and calories, two things I haven't gotten enough of in the last week. If recent events have told me anything, it's that I should make a point to stay replenished, as there is a strong likelihood I'm going to soon be needing it.

Just as my years in the military have instilled, always consume when the opportunity presents itself. One never knows when the next chance might arise.

A bottle of water in hand, I lean back in one of the wooden chairs provided for the table in the corner. Perched on the edge of the bed before me is Valerie. Leaning forward, her fingers are laced between her knees, a look of concern on her face.

Behind her, Fran sits at the head of the bed, her back against the wall, staring off into space.

"How much English?" I ask, leaving my question vague.

"None," Valerie replies, catching where I was going with that. "I mean, no more than basic greetings, anyway."

Nodding slightly, I ask, "And you?"

Again, I am speaking in fragments, hoping she will know where I am leading.

"Was born here," she says. "They sent my father here for college, he never went back."

Like me, she is speaking in code, trusting that I will fill in the blanks.

"And him? Now?"

"Gone," she says.

Flashing my gaze to the head of the bed, I ask, "Same?"

"No, but yes."

Words have been sparing, but they provide a great deal of clarity to the situation. Decades before, Fran Ogo sent her son to America. Allowed entry under COFA, he was either sick at the time or contracted it later on, eventually succumbing to cancer.

Not thyroid, but some form of it, a result of spending his formative years with such direct exposure to the radiation still in the area.

"I'm sorry," I whisper. "For both of them."

Pressing her lips tight together, Valerie nods slightly. "Thank you for getting the medicine. It isn't much, but it does help."

My turn to nod, I accept her thanks, before saying, "The house is still under surveillance. Two men, plain car. Not the same as last night, but from the same group."

"The same group that..." she says, using a hand to motion toward me.

"Yes," I reply. They are from the Wolves, the same people that killed my wife, that seem intent on turning the lives of so many other people upside down.

People that at first glance don't seem to be connected, or at least not enough to warrant what is happening.

"I spoke to the doctor. He told me he had never met my wife."

"No, he hadn't," Valerie replies. "We only met her a couple of times."

Falling silent, I chew on that a moment, trying to make sense of it.

"Walk me through it," I say, my focus shifted to the side, still trying to put these women and my wife together. "Who called who? How was this all set up?"

The basic backbone for what brought them along was there. Fran Ogo was a COFA migrant that was sick and needed care. My wife was a social worker that specialized in helping people navigate the system.

Still, there were large gaps that existed between almost every aspect, different spheres floating nearby, but not yet overlapping.

"Do you happen to know a woman named Mallory Rueben?"

The name surprises me, my eyebrows rising. "I know Mallory very well. She's the one that let me into my wife's office, which is how I got your name and contact information."

The response is a small bastardization of events, but by and large it is the truth. I'm not lying about anything, though perhaps omitting just a bit.

"Right, well, I went to undergrad with her," Valerie replies. "Not terribly close, more like Facebook friends. She was a bit older, already had a family to get home to each night."

Nodding, I remain silent, letting her continue.

"When Nana got the diagnosis and the doctor told us we were going to need to seek out specialized care, I guess I kind of freaked out. I'm a graduate student and work part-time.

"I have insurance through school, have a little money from when Papa died, but..."

Cutting herself off, I can see the overhead lights reflecting off the sheen of moisture in her eyes. What she is describing is difficult, the sort of thing thousands of people in the country experience every day.

Healthcare is absurdly expensive, cancer treatment of any kind even more so. Trying to do that as a migrant that doesn't speak English, or even Spanish, is almost impossible.

"And she recommended Mira?" I ask. My voice is no more than a whisper, my core tightening. I hate the idea that one of our friends might have in some tiny way contributed to what happened to her, no matter how unknowing.

Even more what it would do to Mallory if she ever found out.

"She did," Valerie replies. "Said Mira was the healthcare guru in the office, that if anybody could get us squared away, it would be her."

To see Dana Penson on the street, a person's most immediate thought would be soccer mom. *Not meant to be the least bit disparaging, it wasn't even an assessment based solely on looks.*

Sure, she was diminutive in stature, with curly hair that hung almost to her shoulders and a round face positioned above a rounder torso, but it was based more on her demeanor. On the fact that her voice was almost singsong. That she never used a swear word, instead preferring to exclaim fiddlesticks, *or* phooey, *or even* rats *if things really weren't going her way.*

Or that the scrubs she wore were always festooned with Garfield or Sponge-Bob or some other such character.

Or a thousand other tiny things that made her who she was.

All of which made the fact that she was making my life miserable, rendering me in agony virtually at will, all the more difficult to swallow.

"I told you you weren't ready for eight yet," Dana said, her voice bearing just the slightest bit of self-satisfaction.

Bent over at the waist, drawing in massive breaths of air, all I could see was the bright white of the running shoes she wore, though I had no doubt if I looked up, the expression to match her tone would be plastered across her face.

With one hand draped over the steel railing beside me, I glanced to the rubber-coated eight-pound dumbbell on the ground between my feet. Less than half the size of either shoe I wore, I stared at it with disdain before pulling myself upright.

As I did so, the full light of the outside world returned hit me square, the morning sun made even brighter as it reflected off the three inches of fresh snowfall we'd received overnight.

Despite the frigid scene depicted on the other side of the window, sweat ran down over my face, saturating the stray hairs sprawled across my forehead. The salty brine of it rested flush on my lips, adding to the frustration I felt.

"I told you, I'm not doing the fives anymore," I said, keeping my face turned from Dana, my eyes squinted up as I stared outside.

Positioned on the far end of campus, the rehab facility backed up to an open field that was ran by the agricultural department. Some months prior, it had been planted with winter wheat, the snow having settled into even rows lined across it, promising to be knee-high by July 4th.

As a former athlete, I was granted access to the facility for as long as was necessary, needing only to make a couple of phone calls to put things in motion. Since I was still an employee of the Red Sox, they were footing the bill for everything, making it an arrangement that worked well for all parties.

The training center was well compensated for their time. I was allowed to be where I wanted, living with the person I needed. Everything was good.

Except for the fact that my recovery was taking much, much longer than I'd anticipated.

"Aw, come on," Dana said, coming up alongside me. Resting her palms against the same steel bar I was leaning against, her wrists flush against her chest, she added, "You can't let the fact that they're pink push you off."

Flicking my gaze to the mirrors running the length of the room beside us, I could see the faint smile on her features, knew that she was only joking with me.

Though that did nothing to dampen the frustration roiling through me.

"I don't give a damn if they're made of cotton candy," I snapped. "It's the fact that we've been at this for almost two months, and a damn eight-pound dumbbell is kicking my ass."

Beside me, I could see a flash of dark hair as she looked my way, her jaw parting slightly.

"Look, Kyle," she said, the melodic lilt of her voice receding as she looked my way, "I know this is hard. And that it takes a lot longer than you'd like-"

"But what? I have to keep at it? I have to forget about the fact that spring training opens in three weeks and I still can barely pick up a dumbbell that weighs a fraction of what a bat does?"

My mouth open, there was no less than a dozen – two dozen – things I wanted to add. Bits of venom I wanted to fling, aiming it at everything I could think of.

Myself for having dove at that damn ball. My shoulder for taking so long to come around. The surgeon for not doing a better job. Dana for not making it better already.

None of this was how things were supposed to be. Coming back to Corvallis was a choice, somewhere to train with the team through the winter months before heading to Florida in February to try my hand with the big team.

Not this. None of this.

Leaning forward, I raised my face toward the ceiling. I blew a long sigh out through my nose, my eyes sliding closed.

"I'm sorry," I whispered. "I'm just frustrated."

Chapter Twenty-Seven

As the head of the Wolves, Ringer spends the vast majority of his time at The Wolf Den. He, along with his deputies, receive a salary for being there, taking a cut of membership dues and assorted other enterprises that the club is involved in. Not a huge cut, but enough to keep him fed and clothed.

And pay the bills on his own home, the place he retreats to in the moments between stints at the bar.

Even he can't be around the guys all the time.

The reason for his return home tonight has nothing to do with needing a break. He isn't hungry, doesn't want to catch the latest episode of *NCIS,* doesn't even need sleep.

What he needs are answers. And the only way to get them is to have a conversation without a dozen other Wolves listening to the phone call he's about to make.

The home he rents is just outside of Santee, the next town north in order from El Cajon. Far enough removed from the bar to not to be in direct sightline, it is a small dwelling carved into the side of a canyon wall. The front protrudes out, raised on stilts, with a wooden porch lining it. The rear and sides are literally the limestone of the rock formation.

Facing south, the place stays cool year-round, never receiving direct sunlight.

And more importantly, is easy to fortify and defend, with only a single point of entry.

Stepping over the threshold into the house, Ringer flips on the lights, a filmy glow springing to life, illuminating everything. Moving fast, he tosses his keys onto the table by the wall, knowing he won't be here long.

The place is designed as one enormous studio. The size of a regular home, it was built without interior walls, both to take advantage of the unique geographical design and to give him clear sightlines to everything in the home at any time.

As head of the Wolves, he isn't foolish enough to believe that the list of people that would like to see harm befall him isn't lengthy. Everyone from rival crews to past business associations to some members of his own club that might be gunning for a promotion could stop by unannounced.

And when they did, he needs to know he was never more than a few feet from one of the weapons he has stowed around the place. That he could get off a clear shot before they even got their bearings.

In the far back corner is his sleeping area, which consists of a king-sized bed and a miniature gun locker disguised as a night stand. Across from it is a kitchen with all the requisite pieces, though the fridge and the coffee pot are the sole items that ever get used.

Most of the front of the place is left open, a couch and recliner on one-side offset by a table and chairs on the other. A toilet and free-standing shower are tucked along the side.

Otherwise, the place is barren. No pictures on the walls, no throw pillows on the couch or bed.

A head-on collision of a crash pad and a bachelor spread, the place is utilitarian in a way that trends well past Spartan.

Just as Ringer likes it.

Striding across the room, he is still fuming. Taking long steps, he goes straight for the refrigerator, jerking the door open in search of a beer. When none turns up, he sets his attention on a bottle of water, snapping it out and emptying it in one long pull.

When it is empty, he chucks it in the sink before grabbing another and slamming the door shut, leaving a menagerie of old and molding food behind.

In his years as the top man, never before have the cops had the temerity to set foot inside The Wolf Den. More than once they have stopped by, or pulled one of them to the side of the road to ask a few questions, but never have they actually entered.

Certainly not sauntered in as if they belonged there, smugness and condescension rolling off them.

The mere recollection of the black bastard with his sunglasses and tie makes Ringer's blood boil, his grip tightening on the bottle of water in his hand, threatening to blast the cap off the end of it.

Keeping it clamped tight in his paw, he walks over and deposits himself on the couch, a thin plume of dust rising around him. Extracting his phone, he scrolls to the third entry in order and hits send.

"Don't you even think about ignoring me, you bitch," he grumbles, listening to a pair of rings before the line is picked up.

"I told you this afternoon I would be in touch," Elsa Teller says. She doesn't use a greeting of any kind. Her tone makes it clear she'd rather not be having the conversation.

Which is exactly how Ringer feels as well.

"Yeah, well, things have changed since then."

A moment passes, Teller most likely considering what was said, before she asks, "Lincoln? Did he turn up?"

"Nope," Ringer says, "but it's funny you should jump straight to him, because the damn cops showed up today sniffing around about him."

In response, there is nothing but silence. Deciding to wait her out, Ringer leans forward, the phone pressed to his face, his elbows resting on his knees.

The pose isn't nearly as intimidating over the phone, but it does eventually drive home the intended message.

"What? And you think I put them on to you?" Teller asks.

"Seems mighty odd," Ringer replies, "in the course of twenty-four hours, you show up, two of my guys get jumped, and now the cops are coming around. You do the math."

A sharp snort rings out, the sound acerbic, doing nothing to cool the acrimony seeping into Ringer's system. "And you think I walked into your bar, made a business arrangement with you, and then met with you a second time today just to tip law enforcement?

"Leave the math to me. It clearly isn't your strong suit."

Using his elbows, Ringer pushes against his knees, leveraging himself to his feet. He flings the water bottle behind him, sending it bouncing off the couch, every breath loud and angry.

"Listen, woman-"

"Kyle Clady," she says, cutting him off before he can get another word out.

The skin around his eyes creases into tight folds as Ringer pauses. "What?"

"The man you're looking for, the one that put down your guys last night, is likely who did in Mike Lincoln," Teller says, "his name is Kyle Clady. He has a house in Clairemont Mesa."

Ringer isn't sure what he was expecting when he made the call. He'd thought she would hem and haw again, trying to buy more time, keeping them at arm's length. That's part of why he chose to head home to contact her. He didn't want the others witnessing what he had to go through to extract what they needed.

Never once did he expect it to be so easy, for a name to come tumbling out.

"And how long have you known about this?" he asks.

"Does it matter?" she replies.

It did matter. A lot. It could have allowed them to circumvent everything that happened the night before, maybe even the visit from the cops that afternoon.

But the time for such things has passed. Right now, the men were just as angry as he was about the intrusion that afternoon, and they needed somewhere to aim it.

For the time being, Kyle Clady would do.

"Give me the address."

Chapter Twenty-Eight

AFTER ONLY A COUPLE of hours of sleep in the preceding days, I can feel myself flagging. I have forced down food when I could, made myself drink water, but there is truly no way to get around the fuel that is rest.

Especially when already working to tamp down the emotions that I am, trying to move past the most cataclysmic shift my life has ever known.

Twenty minutes ago, I left the Ogo's in their room to eat dinner and watch TV and do whatever else they would like. I offered to drive them anywhere they needed to go, but both declined, whatever bits of stir crazy they might have felt evaporated by the knowledge that there were still men sitting outside their house.

With the new information from Valerie still ping-ponging through my brain, I went to my room and fell back on the bed, the aging mattress seeming to mold itself around me. Staring at the last bits of daylight stretched across the textured ceiling, I thought of how much the day had yielded, and how much still left to be uncovered.

For the first time since my wife's death, I felt like I was getting ahead. Not enough to call it a full foothold, but a toehold at the very least.

Somewhere out there was a list of people that needed to be eliminated. My wife was on it. Fran Ogo was on it. Who else might be, I don't know.

Serving as the triggermen for it are the Wolves. Whether it is through a vested interest of their own or if they are merely holding the guns, I also don't know.

Sure as hell don't know who hired them if their only job is to act as paid assassins.

What I do know is how Mira and the Ogo women first met. What their mutual interest was. And that it was so narrow, there is no other possible explanation for their interaction.

The only reason they could be lumped in together as targets is because of the case they were working together. Or were about to begin working. Or had started to discuss working.

Tomorrow, I will call Mallory. I'll talk to her about referring Mira to the Ogo's, see if I can get her to dig around on other cases like theirs that might have come through the office. I should also call my friends and give them an update. Let them know that I am here, that I appreciate all they've done, that we should all get some much-needed rest.

Not tonight, though. Tonight, I have enough in me for one more phone call, one more point of contact, before drifting off to sleep.

Lying flat on my back, I slide my phone from my front jeans pocket. The light of the front screen is bright inside the darkening room, my eyes squeezing tight in a wince as I stare at the screen, scrolling through my address book.

Needing to go no further than a couple of entries, I find what I am looking for and hit send, putting the call on speakerphone and dropping it onto my chest.

After a handful of rings, it is picked up, the voice on the other end low and contained.

"Hello?" Angelique says

"Hey," I reply, "how's he doing?"

A long sigh is the first response. She sounds exhausted, and for a moment, a surge of guilt passes through me as I consider that I am already in bed and she is still sitting at the hospital.

Especially when the root cause of it is my fault.

"He is okay," she replies. "They are going to discharge him in the morning, just want to give it a few more hours of observation first."

"Good," I reply. "So he's been awake, spirits are good?"

"Awake, yes," Angelique replies. "He keeps asking me what happened last night, what you've found out today. Just like the rest of us, he's confused and worried. Just wants this to be finished so she can be at peace."

She doesn't add anything further, but there is zero need to. I know who she is referring to and what she means, the same thoughts having gone through my head many times.

Right now, Mira is still in holding at the coroner's office. And she will stay there until this is finished. Only then can we lay her to rest knowing her spirit will be unburdened.

Just like only then will we be able to truly mourn her passing, instead of these isolated bursts that we've all been dealing with for the past few days.

"Do you need anything tonight? Food or clothes or anything?"

"No," Angelique says, another sigh evident in her voice, "but thank you for asking. I just had dinner, and I'm going home in the morning. I'll be okay until then."

I begin to respond, but she barrels past it, continuing unabated.

"You get some rest. I'll see you tomorrow."

Bidding her farewell, I punch off the call, leaving the phone on my chest. My eyelids begin to sag as I lay sprawled in the center of the bed, precious sleep creeping over me.

It never actually arrives.

Chapter Twenty-Nine

THE PARAMETERS WERE LEFT QUITE vague on purpose. Byrdie knows that, recognizing it for what it is, a nod of silent appreciation the best he could offer Ringer on their way out the door.

They had a name and address. If not for the man that had put down Linc, then at the very least the one they had encountered the night before. He and Gamer were to go to that spot, they were to find him, and they were to make a statement.

What that was or how it was delivered was not spelled out, which Byrdie knew was the point.

After getting his ass handed to him the night before, this was his chance to make amends, to save face with the other members.

He will not let the opportunity pass.

The mood inside The Wolf Den was aggressive as they'd departed. Every man inside the room was on their feet, ready to ride off into the night, to assert the full weight of the club down on the man that had dared offend them.

The only things that had stopped them were Ringer and a bit of common sense, the address in Clairemont Mesa much too residential for such a thing. If the guy lived alone in Julian or on a hillside in Fallbrook, perhaps, but not in one of the more densely populated neighborhoods in the city.

The law had already showed up once on the day. Riding out in force would almost invite them back for a follow-up visit.

Rising from their spot in the corner, Byrdie and Gamer had been given nothing short of a hero's sendoff. Slaps on the back and yells of encouragement had accompanied them all the way to the door, the men formed into two long lines for their departure.

By the time they had climbed into the car, Byrdie could feel adrenaline coursing through his system. Veins stood out along his arms, goose pimples lining his skin.

The man – the one they called Clady – was good. The night before, he had sniffed out Byrdie's arrival, wrested his gun away, and gotten the better of him.

But it wasn't situational. Byrdie had been careless. He'd been focused on the women.

It wouldn't happen again.

Tucked back into the passenger seat of the same sedan, Byrdie stares out. He lets the events of the night before, of the scene in the bar, play through his head on loop, feeding his internal furnace.

Outside the city lights of Clairemont Mesa file by. Strip malls and shopping centers sit close to the roadway, neon beckoning people forward, standing vivid against the dark sky.

The only sound is Gamer's cellphone between them, a digitized voice telling them when to turn next.

Flicking his gaze toward the screen, Byrdie can see the red dot denoting their final destination grow closer. His heart rate takes another uptick, his hand tightening around his newly-acquired P239, his former one lost in the scuffle the night before.

Following orders, Gamer hooks a left. He pushes them past an elementary school and into a middle-class neighborhood, the bustle of urban sprawl falling away behind them. Gone are any gas stations or bank branches, replaced by single-family dwellings, almost all of them built in the traditional Mission style.

Again, Byrdie flicks his gaze to the screen. They are getting close. He can feel it.

Make a statement. Those were the instructions.

Byrdie plans to do that and then some.

Chapter Thirty

Mira's hand is nestled in the crook of my arm. Her head lays against my shoulder, the smell of her shampoo filling my nostrils. The sound of her heels clicking against the sidewalk provides a soundtrack as we move forward together.

Even in the ethereal state between awake and asleep, my mind immediately goes to that moment. It's like a computer program returning to the same place after a reboot, my new baseline for the last second that anything in the world made sense.

My Mira and I, together, walking along. My last night as an active duty SEAL. Our first chance to truly begin planning and discussing all the things we've been kicking around for years now.

Having seen the montage hundreds of times before, my fingers claw at the comforter I am laying on. My heartrate increases, body temperature rising.

Except, this time I don't make it all the way to the end. I am spared having to witness the single worst moment of my life just once in exchange for something equally unexpected.

And nowhere near as catastrophic, though certainly in the top five.

The phone is still lying on my chest. Right where it was when I signed off the phone with Angelique, it begins to buzz, vibrating against my sternum. Needing no more than a pair of pulses to pull me from the dream state, my eyes pop open, the light of the screen casting a faint pallor across the ceiling.

Beyond it, full darkness has now settled in, the details of the room around me barely visible.

Raising the phone from my chest, the glare of the screen is almost blinding. It sears through my skull, a wince pulling at my features.

Taking a moment to focus, I stare down at it, looking at the string of numbers scrawled across it, no name saved for the contact.

No part of me wants to answer. Right now, I just want to rest. I want to put the last week aside, replenish myself, and then plunge straight ahead again with first light.

But I can't do that. I cannot ignore a local number, not with so much going on, so many different balls in the air, all involving people that I barely know.

"Hello?" I manage, the grogginess I feel permeating my voice.

"Is this Kyle?!"

It is a woman's voice. I don't recognize it right off, but I can tell she is standing outside, a bit of wind moving through the mouthpiece.

I can also tell she is on the verge of hysteria, which in turn activates my own physiology. Pressing the phone tight to my face, I sit straight up, my head spinning slightly before leveling out.

"It is. Who is this?"

"This is Bethany Stanson," she says. "I live across the street from you."

She doesn't need to add the last sentence. I know Bethany, and I know where she lives. Not well enough to have her number in my phone, but enough I don't need the added explanation.

Extraneous information is a classic sign of someone being nervous. Coupled with the fact that each word is louder than the one before, I slide to the edge of the bed and take my feet. I'm already dressed, my gaze moving over the room, searching for my keys.

Something is off, I know it before she says a word.

"What's wrong?" I ask.

"You need to get here now. Your house is on fire."

Chapter Thirty-One

THE WORDS RING in my head. Time and again they sound off, spurring me forward through the night. My house is on fire. The last place I ever shared with my Mira. The bastion for all of our memories and possessions.

The red needle on the speedometer before me nudges north of eighty miles an hour, though I make no effort to slow down as I speed toward town. In the distance, I can see various lights standing out against the night sky. Most are probably nothing more than ballfields or shopping centers, though I can't help but imagine them as the ominous glow of my home being reduced to embers.

Leaning forward in the front seat, I grip the wheel in both hands, practically willing the car forward. I push as hard on the gas as I dare, getting pulled over right now the one thing in the world I can't afford.

Not because I care what a patrolman might think or say, but because I can't sacrifice the time it would take to deal with them.

Uncurling my right hand from around the wheel, I reach to the middle console. I grab my phone and press a single button, balancing it on the top of the wheel.

"Call Swinger."

A small button tone lets me know the order has been received and is being acted upon. In my periphery, I can see the face on the phone shift as the call is connected, the sound of ringing filling the car a moment later.

On the freeway around me, traffic is mercifully thin. Late in the evening on a weeknight, the after-work crowd has fallen away without much of a nighttime pool to fill in behind them. A few businesses along the road have already gone dark, locking their doors for the night.

I would love nothing more than to be doing that same thing. To be still laying in that bed at the Valley View, or better yet at home with Mira in the house that is now being reduced to rubble.

The phone rings a second and a third time as my mind settles on the simple fact that I moved out into the desert because I wasn't yet up to facing the house and all it represented. I had tried a handful of times, never making it more than a few minutes alone before it all became too much.

"Yeah," Swinger answers. In the background is noise, most likely out for a nightcap.

Not that it will matter. He's never not shown for me. Just like I will always do the same for him.

"They torched it," I say, skipping past most of an explanation. "The sonsabitches torched our house."

All sound fades away, a few muffled movements the only noise, punctuated by a car door slamming shut.

"Who?" he asks.

"I don't know," I reply. And I don't know, though I have a pretty good idea. "Neighbor called a few minutes ago."

"How bad?"

"Not sure," I say. "Driving in town now."

There is a pause. Right now, I know my friend Jeff Swinger is buried beneath the surface, my colleague Chief Swinger taking over. He is taking a moment, analyzing what we know, considering things from every angle.

"Could be a trap," he says. "They've been on the place, seen you haven't been back."

I had the same thought shortly after pulling away from the motel. "Yeah," I agree.

"You still carrying?"

On the passenger seat beside me is the Mark 23. It catches a bit of ambient light as I pass beneath a highway stanchion pole, a tangerine hue sliding over its polished surface.

"Yeah."

"Good," he replies. "I'm rolling now. Don't do anything until one of us gets there."

He doesn't clarify who *us* refers to, and he doesn't tell me to call anybody else.

Just like I sign off without telling him that my house isn't where I'm headed right now.

At least, not at first.

———

The sound of the party greeted us the moment we stepped out of the car. Echoing well beyond the outer walls of the home in Southwest, it was a mixture of music and voices, the low din of conversation punctuated by the occasional spike of laughter.

Accompanying the sound was a burst of light, bright glow pushing through the windows lining the first floor of the home, shining like a beacon into the darkness.

"You know you don't actually have to do this," Mira said. Exiting from the passenger side of the car, she met me on the curb by the front headlight, a hand extended.

Slipping her fingers through mine as I approached, she gave them a squeeze, two quick pulses relaying dozens of different sentiments.

All of which were appreciated.

"What? Why wouldn't I want to do this?" I asked. "This is your big night."

This time, it was my turn to squeeze her hand, using the grip to pull her my way. Remaining on the street alongside the curb, I pulled her closer, the extra four inches it provided her bringing us nose-to-nose with one another.

Making no effort to stop me, Mira allowed her stomach to press tight against mine, the puffy coats we both wore providing an inch of space between us.

"No," Mira replied, "my big night was a week ago, and you were there for that. That's all that matters."

Even as she said words, I knew they were more for my benefit than hers.

"That's ridiculous," I replied. "I mean, yes, actually winning the national championship was a big deal, but this is too."

A flash of white teeth appeared before more, striping through her perpetually tan skin. A puff of warm breath hit me full in the face as she lowered her gaze to the ground, dark hair swinging forward, brushing against my skin.

Tonight was not actually a big deal in the slightest, and we both knew it, each going through the motions, trying to talk ourselves into actually stepping foot inside.

The Oregon State racquetball program was the stuff of legend. Having won nine consecutive national championship, it had become the gold standard in the country, the equivalent of Alabama in football or Iowa in wrestling.

They were without peer, the reason Mira had matriculated north from San Diego to a frigid small town in Oregon.

But that didn't mean they knew much about how to throw a party, whatever athletic acumen they had offset by the occasional shortcoming of social skills.

"No, really," Mira said, "I insist. If you don't want to go in, we don't have to."

A matching smile lit my features as I pulled her a bit closer, just millimeters separating our faces. I released my grip on her hand, instead sliding my hands around her back, locking them just above her hips.

"Well, now, while that is a very noble gesture – and one that will be rewarded handsomely later – I cannot in good conscience have you missing out on the social event of the year on my behalf."

Raising a hand to my face, Mira traced a finger the length of my nose. Continuing to pull it lower, she dragged it over my lips, the feel of it soft against my skin.

"A handsome reward, huh? And what might that entail?"

Opening my mouth to respond, handfuls of answers came to mind, ranging the full spectrum of the rating system. Pausing, I drew in a breath, contemplating how racy to make my response, wondering how much I truly didn't want to go up the front walk and step inside.

"You two going inside, or you just going to stand out here making us gag all night?"

The voice was one we both knew implicitly. In unison, our smiles melted away, our bodies going rigid as we turned over a shoulder.

Where Nancy Raye had come from, neither of us knew. Dressed in a long peacoat, she had a wool hat pulled down over her bushy blonde hair, a plastic sack in hand. The other was pressed into her hip, her body cocked to the side, like a scolding parent having caught two teenagers after curfew.

To say she and I were mortal enemies might be a bit of an over-statement.

Calling us friends definitely would be.

"Hey, Nancy," Mira said, her chin tucked up next to my shoulder. "You just getting here, too?"

Taking a step forward, she dropped the hand from her hip, though the accusatory look remained. "I am, though I seem to be in a little more of a hurry to get inside. Sorry to have interrupted."

It was clear she wasn't. Standing there, I couldn't help but wonder if she'd ever actually been sorry about a thing in her life.

"Didn't expect you to still be around," she said, flicking her gaze from Mira to me. "Just another baseball star that couldn't give it up, huh?"

Chapter Thirty-Two

IT HAS BEEN A BUSY DAY, but a frustrating one. The trip to Mike Lincoln's house was successful only in that Detective Malcolm Marsh had been lucky enough to encounter a nosy neighbor that was all-too-happy to share what she knew.

Marsh hated relying on luck. It was sloppy. Lazy police work, the type of thing that would eventually catch up to him, maybe even become a red flag in his file.

And red flags were something he would not abide. Not with his aspirations.

Discovering Lincoln rode with the Wolves had been a stroke of luck, though the trip to the ragged shack they called a bar had been even less fruitful than his house. Bastards wouldn't even speak directly to him, instead enlisting their lackey bartender to serve as a mouthpiece.

As clear a statement as to what they thought of him and his investigation as anything there could be.

In the wake of it, he and Tinley had driven back to the precinct, neither saying much, each working through the new information in their own way. For his partner, that meant scribbling down notes, drawing lots of circles and arrows, trying to ferret out patterns and connections that may or may not exist

For Marsh, that meant staring out through the windshield, letting his growing vitriol simmer, working through each piece of information he had.

This had all started with Mira Clady, a woman who for some reason was still residing at the coroner's office. In the time since, her Navy SEAL husband had showed up a couple of times, acted openly hostile, and hosted a growing collection of open wounds.

And now, somehow, the Wolves were involved.

Leaning back in his desk chair, Marsh stares at the screen before him. One elbow propped on the arm of his chair, his smooth head is balanced in his palm, his focus on the files fanned wide.

Twenty minutes earlier, Tinley had ducked out to make a food run, their unusual shift altering traditional meal times by more than a couple of hours. Thankful for the silence the errand would provide, Marsh had requested something well beyond the scope of their neighborhood, relishing having the office to himself again.

Just a few days back, and already he is wishing his partner would consider going on another vacation.

The information readily available in the SDPD database on the Wolves is thin. The first mention of them was from eighteen years ago, a single noise complaint that was quickly withdrawn. From there, small notations were made in various reports, witnesses to barfights or minor assaults saying one of the participants was wearing a vest bearing the moniker.

Scrolling through, Marsh can feel his agitation growing. Nowhere is there mention of a member being arrested themselves, nor is there any hard data on total enrollment. Based on the size of the bar and small handful he'd seen, Marsh can't imagine there being more than a couple dozen, though that is purely a guess.

And even at that, more than enough people to wreak some serious havoc.

Leaning forward, Marsh grabs up the receiver on his desk telephone. Dropping it onto the desktop, he pulls up the SDPD internal directory on screen. Finding the listing for the gang unit, he dials the number, glancing to the clock in the bottom corner of the monitor.

It is late, probably too late to speak to somebody, but it's worth a shot. Maybe he will catch someone like himself, another climber not afraid of staying after hours.

Or maybe even one of those do-gooder types he's heard about but never encountered himself, someone that chips away night after, working in vain to make a difference.

Leaving the phone on speaker, he listens as it rings a handful of times. Just as expected, it goes to voicemail.

Smirking, Marsh lifts the receiver and says, "Good evening, this is Detective Malcolm Marsh, Central Precinct. I'm calling to get any information you might have on a motorcycle outfit working out of El Cajon called The Wolves."

Finishing by leaving his contact information, the phone is barely back in its cradle as he hears the front door to the precinct burst open. The sound of pounding footsteps grows closer, heavy footfalls slapping against the floor, culminating with Tinley appearing before him.

Pitched forward, he has either side of the doorway in his hands, his breath coming in ragged bursts.

"Just heard on the scanner," he said, "major home fire in Clairemont Mesa."

Taking a moment, Marsh considers the news. Nothing comes to him.

"So?" he asks.

"So, it's at the address of Kyle Clady."

Chapter Thirty-Three

IT IS my third time traveling the route in just over twenty-four hours. At this point I know it well enough that I wind my way through rote memory, not needing directions or to really even pay attention where I'm going.

My hands just seem to know the way, feeding off my subconscious mind.

Occupying the front of my mind is a montage of images from my home. One after another, they scroll through, tendrils of red and orange climbing into the sky, decimating what little I have remaining of my wife.

The furniture, my clothes, anything in the garage – those things I can live without.

The photos? Her clothes? The bed we shared? The dog collar on the counter in the hallway? Her smell?

The million memories all tucked away?

The mere thought of them being reduced to cinders pulsates through me. My eyes burn, hot with angry tears, the imagined smell of smoke filling my nostrils.

And belying it all is hate. Pure, unadulterated, rage. The type of emotion that I have been trained for a decade to suppress. The instantaneous response that we are always told to avoid, as it occurs without forethought and often leads somewhere bad.

But I don't care. As mama always told me growing up, it takes a real asshole to start a fight, but there is no shame in ending one.

Where I'm headed now won't end this one, but it'll damn sure make my intentions to do so clear.

The neighborhoods of Chula Vista are largely quiet as I turn off the freeway. At such an hour in the middle of the week, that is to be expected. Dinner is over and families have put their children to bed, winding down in front of the television or preparing for sleep themselves.

It is a snapshot of what life is supposed to be like. What mine looked like a week ago. What I was planning on it looking like for the next fifty years.

Clamping my jaw tight, I find Camino del Reine and turn north. I flip the front headlights to bright, hoping to throw a little extra glare on anybody that might be looking my way, as I idle forward. Rotating my head to either side, I scan every vehicle sitting on the street, looking for my target.

To my right, the Ogo home slides past, windows darkened, not a soul around since I slipped out the back hours before.

I barely give it a glance, the home not what I've come for tonight.

That I find parked toward the end of the street.

Sitting on the left side, the pair of heads silhouetted through the front windshield are as obvious as flashing lights. Falling under the glow of my front lamps, one raises a hand to block the glare, the other looking away.

Neither makes any move to climb out.

Reaching into the passenger seat, I grab the Mark 23 and slide it up onto my thigh. I take the wheel in my right hand, my left gripping the base of the gun.

The engine I let continue to idle forward, closing the gap between us.

Adrenaline and anticipation pass like pinpricks the length of my body. The scabs on my hand and upper arm itch, every nerve ending knowing what is coming.

I have spent ten years as an active duty SEAL in the employee of the United States government. I have been trained in every form of combat known to man, have employed those skills in a myriad of locations and operations around the globe.

There is no way to know for certain how many lives I have taken. All I know is that every one was done under direct orders, each intent to do the same to me if given the chance.

Five days ago was the first time I had ever taken a life on domestic soil. Damned sure the first time I went after someone that wasn't armed and firing back at me.

This will make twice.

Nudging the wheel to the left, I close the gap between the row of cars parked along the curb and the side of my sedan to just few a couple of feet. Lowering the driver's side window, I can feel the cooling air of outside rush in, wrapping around me. It touches at the sweat on my face, sending palpitations the length of my skin.

Not once do I hesitate, letting the car move until drawn even with the men sitting in the car, my window parallel to theirs, before hitting the brakes. At the sight of me pulling to an abrupt stop, the pair of men sharing the front seat both turn my way, scowls in place.

Occupying the driver's seat is a man in his mid-forties, his hair buzzed short, a blonde goatee framing his mouth. An earring hangs from his left lobe as he turns to me, gold tooth glinting as he starts to say something.

I never hear a word of it.

Stretching my arm out through the open window, the bullet has no more than a foot or two to travel, most of the sound swallowed by the suppressor screwed down on the end of the barrel. Hitting him square between the eyes, the back part of his skull explodes out at an angle, plastering the rear window with blood. Brain and bone matter both speckle the back seat.

The momentum of the shot tosses him back against the seat, his body wedged beneath the wheel, propped upright by the narrow confines of the car.

In the passenger seat, a man that looks to be no more than a couple of years past thirty stares at me. His eyes wide, he slowly raises his hands, blood spatter covering his left arm and his cheek, shining against the dark hair hanging just past his chin.

His lower mandible quivers, though no sounds come out.

That is a good thing. If I have to hear a word from him, I may not have the self-control not to keep firing.

"So you guys like to watch old women? Burn down houses in the middle of the night?" I ask. My voice is even and measured. The gun remains extended out through the open window, aimed directly at the man in the passenger seat.

The scent of gunpowder fills my nostrils. It gives me a sense bordering on euphoria, practically urging me to fire again. And again. And again.

But I can't. I need this guy alive. I need him to wrestle his buddy into the back seat and drive away the evidence of what just happened.

I need him to deliver a message back to The Wolf Den.

"Tell your guys I didn't start this, damned sure didn't want it." I pull the gun back inside. "But I'm not going anywhere."

Chapter Thirty-Four

THERE IS a carnival atmosphere surrounding my house that I first spotted more than a mile out. Rising bright above the cityscape, it is a combination of orange glow and the rotating lamps of first-responder vehicles, a menagerie of colors drawing me in.

Just seeing it, any animosity I felt in Chula Vista ebbs away, replaced by the emotion I was feeling when I first got the call. Moisture returns to my eyes, my heart palpitating as I push as close as the gathered assemblage of vehicles and onlookers will allow. Parked at haphazard angles, they block the entire intersection onto my street, the world awash in red and blue flashers.

Nudging the front of my car to the side of the road, I pull the keys and jump out, barely swinging the door shut in my wake. The smell of wood smoke hits me full as I run forward, sweat and tears both lining my cheeks. My lungs fight for air against my sprint and the thick smog in the air, a cacophony of sound filtering in around me.

On the entire drive in from El Cajon, and again on the way up from Chula Vista, my mind had been filled with images. Thoughts of my home serving as an enormous bonfire, flames blazing high, red and yellow and orange all like fingers, reaching upward for the sky.

That's what I had expected. What I had braced myself for.

What I found was so much worse.

The half-hour since Bethany Stanson called me was more than enough for the fire to tear through my home. No longer is it an upright structure for flames to chew through with aplomb. Instead, it is nothing more than a frame, the studs glowing bright, the rest of the place already stripped away.

Around the outside of the property sits a trio of fire trucks, fighters aiming their hoses toward it. From the tips of all three spouts a heavy torrent of water, but at this point it is nothing more than damage control, making sure nothing else along the block gets consumed as well.

The house is gone. As is everything in it.

Every memento I have of my wife. Every shared item I had hoped to keep for the rest of my days.

Threading my way through the mass of people and vehicles, I stop in the middle of the street. I raise my hands to my head, lacing my fingers atop my skull, making no effort to stop the various forms of moisture that slide down my cheeks.

Standing there, locked in that position, I have no concept of my surroundings, no awareness of who might be nearby. I barely notice as a hand finds the small of my back, Stapleton stepping up beside me. As another one squeezes my shoulder, Swinger appearing on my opposite flank.

Somewhere close by, or on in his way in, is Ross I'm sure. My friends have been here for me since the moment Mira passed. A long time before that, even.

There is no way they won't be here tonight. And while I am thankful for their presence, I can't begin to say as much right now.

I can't say anything.

The urge to rush forward is so strong I can barely keep it at bay, though I remain rooted in place. I want nothing more than to sprint at the remains of my home, to hurtle over the glowing threshold of the door and save something – *anything* – of my life with Mira. I want to find every man wearing a Wolves vest and toss them headlong into the flames.

I want to stand and scream until my throat is raw. Cry until I have no moisture left in my body. Lash out until every bone in my hand is broken.

Most of all, I want this nightmare to end. I want to wake up with my wife in a world where I don't know the Wolves even exist, where I don't know this kind of pain, where I have some semblance of a plan for the future.

Chapter Thirty-Five

THE DECISION TO burn the man's house to the ground wasn't necessarily what Ringer had in mind when he told Byrdie to make a statement, but he can't argue that the choice was wrong. If given his preference, he would have preferred that it involve some sort of physical harm, but torching his every tangible possession wasn't a bad backup plan.

Besides, after what Clady did to Byrdie the night before, it is a safe bet that if an actual altercation were at all possible, he would have made that happen.

And it's not like they wanted to have a second home to be sitting watch over.

The faint smell of gasoline and smoke lingers on Byrdie and Gamer as they sit to either side of Ringer. Neither looks to be overly joyed to be back at their corner post in The Wolf Den, though they do appear to be much better off than the night before.

This was a victory, albeit a measured one. They still need to find and deal with Clady, they still need to track down the old woman, and they still have to contend with the detectives that showed up that afternoon, but for the first time since Linc went missing, the Wolves can tally a win.

It isn't enough to completely dissipate the hatred Ringer felt earlier while speaking to Teller, but it's a start.

Four tall beer glasses sit on the table before them, a half-dozen wet rings pockmarked across the top of it. Three of the four are less than half-full, Byrdie's barely touched as they sit and debrief.

As best Ringer can tell, Byrdie and Gamer sat on the house for two hours, seeing not a single light or sign of life. Aware of the clock ticking, of the fact that the detectives that had visited them might also be on Clady, they decided to leave their post along the curb.

They pulled directly into his driveway, their movements hidden under cover of darkness. Carrying only a plastic jug of accelerant and a blow torch, Gamer was through the front door in seconds, the thin wooden casing no match for his size and strength.

From there, it was fairly simple. Homes in San Diego were often made from the cheapest materials, designed to allow for maximal air flow. They weren't made to withstand a nuclear blast, the fire chewing through it in record time.

"We gave it fifteen minutes," Gamer says. Leaning forward, his massive fists are wrapped around his mug, one of the knuckles bearing a small scab from the night before. In that position, his shoulders bunch up beneath his neck, a thick roll of fat extended like a ring from ear to ear. "When the sirens started wailing, we decided to get out of there."

Grunting, Ringer nods slightly. "No sign of him?"

"Nope."

"Anybody see you?"

"Definitely not," Gamer replies. A quick glance over to Byrdie is answered with a shake of his head, secondary confirmation that they weren't spotted.

Whether that's true or not, Ringer has no way of knowing right now, figuring they'll find out soon enough.

Leaning back in his seat, he raises a hand to his face. He scratches at the underside of his jaw, nails digging against wiry bristles.

The decision to go after Clady might seem brash, but it was a risk worth taking. After the disappearance of Linc, it could be assumed he already knew about them anyway. After the events of the night before, it was assured.

They had nothing to gain from waiting any longer. It was time for them to get out ahead, to put up a show of force.

To make a statement.

"Okay, good," Ringer replies, thinking ahead, working on the next thing in order.

A thing that never arrives, interrupted by the swinging doors spilling open. Through it tumbles a young man with dark hair hanging around his chin. Barely able to stay upright, he staggers to the bar, just catching himself, before turning wild-eyed toward the corner.

His left arm is painted red with blood, speckles and streaks, all of it dried. Smears line his hands and the front of his jeans.

Recognizing him as Dru, Ringer rises from his seat, the three around him turned and staring. Every other member that is still hanging around does the same, all sound falling away as everybody stares.

Any hint of optimism that existed a moment before is gone.

"It's Clady," Dru says, swinging his gaze around the room, moving past Ringer twice before settling his focus on him. "He got Prince."

Chapter Thirty-Six

ON THE OPPOSITE corner of the property, positioned in the middle of the street, Detective Malcolm Marsh watches as Kyle Clady arrives. Moving like a specter between the various police cruisers and fire trucks, he seems oblivious to the chaos of the world around him, his sole focus on the home.

Where he has been or what has taken him so long to arrive, Marsh hasn't a clue. Shifting from the house, he makes no effort to hide his appraisal as he openly stares at Clady, waiting for his reaction, wanting to see some semblance of how he responds to all this.

When Tinley first told him about the fire, his instinct immediately went to arson. Intentional or not he wasn't sure, though starting a bonfire and trying to purge every memory of a lost loved one wasn't an entirely unheard of way of handling things.

It wasn't likely that would include an entire home, but sometimes things get away from someone. He already knew Clady had been staying elsewhere, had needed some space for the time being.

Seeing his arrival removed all such thoughts. His movements frantic, his responses completely real, there was no way to fake that sort of emotion. No way he would be so late arriving, would have that visceral a reaction, if things were staged.

The fire is real. Whether planned or not, Marsh will have to look into. If so, he will have to determine who did it, if it was the same people that shot Clady's wife, if his visit to The Wolf Den earlier that day was just the first of many.

But all that will have to wait for now.

Even if this is the case that Marsh has been waiting for, that one enormous bust that will be the catalyst he needs out of Imperial Beach and San Diego in general, it will have to at least wait until morning.

Beside him, he feels Tinley tap the back of his wrist. Shifting his chin over a few inches, he sees his partner motion to Clady across the way, his hands raised above his head.

"There he is," Tinley whispers.

Saying nothing, Marsh watches as a woman with red hair steps up beside Clady, a hand on his back. A big man with a sleeve of tattoos falls in on the other side. A black man in long sleeves completes the quartet.

Not one of them says a word, their attention squarely on the house.

Watching them another moment, Marsh puts his hands in his pockets. Shuffling his feet, he turns and looks at the glowing embers of the home, a steady plume of white smoke rising into the air beneath the deluge of water the firefighting teams are cascading over it.

A tiny bit of the original heat has receded, replaced by the smell of smoke so strong it burns the nostrils.

"Come on, let's go," Marsh says. Turning away from the house, he walks in the opposite direction of Clady, toward their sedan parked a block away.

"Wait," Tinley calls.

Marsh doesn't slow, picking his way past first-responders as his partner comes up beside him, jogging to close the gap.

"That's it?" he asks. "We came all this way and we're not even going to question him?"

Glancing over, Marsh shakes his head. "Kyle Clady didn't do this."

"But, still-"

This time, Marsh comes to a complete stop. He turns and looks at Tinley before glancing back at Clady and his friends standing in the street, none having moved an inch.

"I'd say the man's been through enough for one night, wouldn't you?"

————

When I left Corvallis eight months before, Mira had moved into my old place. A small cottage on the outskirts of town, it backed up to the Bald Hill Recreation area, the place the visual depiction of the word idyllic.

On the back porch sat a picnic table and a charcoal grille overlooking a sweeping meadow. Set aside as a cow pasture, most of the year it was a deep shade of green or gold, a herd of grazing black angus roaming lazily across it, perpetually in search of their next meal.

Tired of dorm living, she had asked the older couple I rented from if she could take over.

Considering she basically lived there already, they were more than amenable to the idea, even welcoming me back when I returned several months later.

For all but the short spell I was in Massachusetts, and Arizona or Montana the summers before that, the place had been where I lived for the last four years, the longest I had ever stayed in a single place. Furnished in a warm, comfortable style, it was the place in the world I was most at ease.

But even at that, sitting in the front living room, the lights off, cool air seeping through the rear windows, it no longer felt like home.

Reclined on the couch, stockinged feet extended onto the coffee table before me, crossed at the ankle, I sat with the television off. Staring past the silent black screen, I instead focused on the meadow out back, on the thick blanket of white covering it, moonlight refracting off the surface.

So locked in thought, deep in the recesses of my own mind, I didn't hear Mira approach. Didn't even know she was there until she slid a hand across my shoulder, circling around the sofa.

The springs beneath us shifted slightly as she dropped down beside me, the warmth and grog of sleep still clinging to her. Resting her head against my shoulder, her long hair fell against my neck, her hands sliding into the crook of my elbow and pulling it over.

For more than a minute, neither of us said a thing, each staring out, the quiet not quite awkward, but certainly not comfortable either.

Per usual, it was Mira that worked up the nerve to go first.

"You can't let what Nancy said get to you. She's always had a thing. You know that."

Whether she was referring to the fact that her teammate had a major inferiority complex for all things Oregon State baseball or at one time had had romantic interest in me, I couldn't be sure.

Nor could I argue that either one would be wrong.

"What makes you think I'm sitting in here thinking about Nancy?" I replied, my tone having far less conviction than I would have liked, knowing she would see right through it.

Though I still had to go through the motions all the same.

A small snort was Mira's first response, her head rocking slightly against my arm. "Because you've barely said ten words since."

Shifting, she turned to look at me, pressing her chin and lips against my arm. Turning for just a moment, I matched her gaze, holding it before shifting and looking back out through the rear window.

Per usual, she was right. I had been unable to sleep and I was sitting in the dark thinking about things, though she was wrong in thinking it was because of Nancy.

Or, at least, just because of Nancy.

"It's just..." I said, losing my voice for a moment as I tried to formulate the best way to proceed. "She's not wrong. I love Corvallis, I love this house, I love being with you..."

Squeezing my arm a bit tighter, Mira prompted, "But?"

"But right now, I feel like I'm in a holding pattern. Like I'm clinging to a life that's gone. Like everything else has moved forward, and I'm still stuck staring in the rearview."

Not wanting to fire back too quickly, to refute whatever I was thinking or feeling, Mira nodded. She considered things for a moment, sitting in silence, before saying, "But it's not your fault. You got hurt. You're still healing."

I knew it wasn't my fault. What had happened was a freak accident. The thing that had always made me a good player – the complete abandon I used in all aspects of the game – had ultimately become my undoing.

It was unfortunate, but it was fair.

What wasn't was sitting around, trying to cling to something I knew was getting further away by the day.

"It's been months," I whispered, "and still I can barely swing a whiffle ball bat. Nobody wants to say anything, they keep insisting on being positive and supportive, but I can see the looks in their eyes."

I didn't bother finishing the sentence. Not because I couldn't bring myself to do it, but because there was no need to.

My Mira knew me better than anyone. She had seen me every day since my return, no doubt sensed the thoughts I was carrying around. The self-doubt that was starting to creep in, the realization that what I'd always wanted to do was slowly coming to an end.

And that what scared me most was I had no idea where I went from there.

———

Turn the page for a sneak peek of *Ships Passing*, part 4 of the My Mira Saga, or download now and continue reading: dustinstevens.com/SPam

Sneak Peek

SHIPS PASSING, MY MIRA SERIES BOOK 4

I'M NOT sure how I know. Like the words to a song I haven't heard in ages or the ending of a movie I stumble across late at night on cable, the pattern is already ingrained in my mind, the outcome sealed long before reaching the conclusion.

As if imprinted on me so long before that the origin has ceased being of importance, cast aside into the ethereal abyss that the mind creates for all that it doesn't deem worthy of preserving.

The instant I hear the sound, the clear din of an engine approaching, every nerve ending in my body draws taut. My senses sharpen, picking up on the slightest shifts around me.

The diminishing light inside the room. The weak rattle of an air conditioning unit from next door. The smell of dust and cleaning product in the air.

Perched on the edge of the bed, I sit ramrod straight, counting off seconds. A sheen of sweat covers my skin, the residual light of day reflecting from it, though I am not nervous.

The point for that has come and gone.

Nor am I angry. Or sad. Or really feeling much of anything beyond the tiniest bit of relief, knowing that this inevitability was coming. In a way, I'm just glad to get it over with, to put this behind me forever.

Fingers splayed over the tops of my thighs, I hear as the brakes moan slightly, bringing the approaching vehicle to a halt. As the engine cuts out a moment later.

As a door wrenches open and footsteps crunch across the parking lot, the mixture of dirt and gravel allows each one to ring out. Hearing them, I am able to track my visitor's movement, imposing them on the images in my mind, knowing exactly where they stand at any given moment.

My breathing increases slightly, my pulse picking up, thrumming through my temples. Still, I remain motionless on the edge of the bed, watching as a shadow passes by the threadbare curtain hanging over the window at the front of the room.

It is time.

Finally.

———

Hours have passed since I first showed up to see my home standing as a fiery pyre, oversized fingers of orange and yellow reaching ever higher into the night sky. In the time since, most of the commotion that was present when I first arrived has subsided.

Many of the first responders have now come and gone. A pair of police cruisers sit at either end of the street. To my right, a pair of officers lean against the front hood, glancing between the house and the street, waving off the occasional rubbernecker that tries to peer down on their way to work.

At the opposite end, the two men have given up the task, instead retreating inside their vehicle, their heads silhouetted behind the windshield.

Not that I harbor any ill will toward them. They are right. There isn't anything more they can do.

Between them, the quartet of fire engines that first showed up has shrunk to a single unit. A small cluster of men in oversized fire-retardant pants and suspenders stand near the back end of it, their bare arms and faces smudged with soot. Spooled out alongside them is enough hose to ensure that the last dying gasps of the home don't somehow spring back to life, but it is clear at a glance that they expect nothing of the sort.

At this point, the fight has been fought and lost.

Just as has almost every earthly possession that remained from my Mira.

When the sun last set, it did so on the definition of a bucolic suburban Southern California neighborhood. Single family dwellings butted up tight to one another, both sides of the street were filled with lots of equal size. Containing all the usual trappings, each had front lawns, side garages, a car or two parked outside.

A few had pets. A smaller handful even had the mythical white picket fence.

Only a matter of hours has passed since then, but already the sun is beginning to rise on a much different scene. No longer does the street look like it once did, an enormous black divot now gouged into the center of it.

What was once my home, the first house my wife and I owned together, the place where we were seriously considering expanding our family, is now nothing but a pile of cinders, each passing moment further reducing all that remains.

By noon, I suspect it will be nothing more than ash, the Santa Ana winds carrying it into the distance.

I can feel the concrete curb beneath me biting into my tailbone as I sit on the opposite side of the street and stare. Disbelief, terror, shock, nostalgia all run through my mind in equal measure. All so fierce, all so prescient, I don't know which to seize on first, my body numb.

For only the second time in my life, I have no idea how to process something.

"Here," a voice says, arriving a split second before a foil package taps against my shoulder. Sliding down a few inches, I can smell sausage and cheese, my hand reaching up to accept the intrusion without my mind truly grasping what it is.

"Breakfast burrito," Wendell Ross says, stepping down onto the street beside me and settling onto the curb.

A fellow Petty Officer, Ross has been by my side since we first went into SEAL training almost a decade before. A bit shorter than me, he is cut from solid muscle, his arms and chest broad plates achieved through hours of bodyweight calisthenics.

Dressed in gym shorts and a long-sleeve neoprene shirt, he places a brown paper bag between his feet as he settles in, though makes no move to open it.

Where he went or how long he's been gone, I can only guess at, the last several hours a menagerie of sights and sounds and thoughts, all of it contorted into one unending nightmare.

Just as the last week since my wife's death as had been.

"You should eat something," Ross says, his voice low and composed. He doesn't bother looking my way as he says it, both of us staring at the shattered remains of the last tangible memories I had of my marriage.

Of course, he is right. Just as he has been a dozen times before over the years when we were together out in the shit, moments when he would ensure the rest of us got the food or rest we needed.

A direct result of being one of the few among us that was also a father, the paternal instinct ingrained.

"Thanks," I manage, not knowing what else to say at the moment.

I do need food. And water. And sleep.

I need to push rewind, and go back to sitting in the corner booth at The Cartwright with Mira and Ross and our friends Emily Stapleton and Jeff Swinger. I need to take her directly home afterward, avoiding Balboa Park and the Wolves and anything else that might endanger her.

I need a lot of things right now. But just like every last one of them, I'm not sure my body can even handle the thought of eating at the moment.

"Jeff and Emily take off?" I whisper.

"Yeah," Ross replies. "They were both going to call in today, but I told them to go on. There's nothing more they can do here."

Again, he is right. There is nothing anybody can do here. In a couple of hours, the fire department will determine that there is no risk of reignition and the police will string crime scene tape across the front. Tomorrow, or the next day, an arson investigator will come out and take a look.

Not that I need to wait that long to know what happened here.

"Sonsabitches," I mutter.

Beside me, Ross grunts slightly. "Wolves?"

Just hearing the name draws my hand up into a fist. My jaw clenches as I stare straight ahead, the burning in my eyes becoming more pronounced.

"Who else?" I whisper.

This time he doesn't bother to respond. There is no need to. We both know who is behind this, the bigger question being the one I've spent much of the last week trying to determine.

Why? Why had one of their members killed my wife in cold blood? Why were they targeting Fran Ogo and her granddaughter Valerie? Why did they search my house six days ago only to come back and burn the place to the ground now?

Why?

The smell of wood char hangs heavy in the air, overpowering even the breakfast in my hand. I haven't caught a glimpse of myself in hours, though I can only imagine how I must appear, with ash and soot staining my cheeks, rivulets streaming vertically through it, revealing where my tears have fallen.

Almost certainly my eyes and nostrils are both red-rimmed, all stinging in the aftermath of the fire.

At this point, I am well past caring.

"What are you thinking?" he asks.

He doesn't expound further, though I know exactly what he is trying to say. He wants to know the plan I'm putting together, wants to make sure I'm not about to do something incredibly stupid.

What he can't possibly understand is, I haven't even made it that far yet, my focus still on the remains of my home before us.

"I have to go in this morning," I reply. "Another one of those damn sessions with the doc."

Pausing, I smirk slightly, the fact that every last thing I have to wear just burned up occurring to me. "Think she'll write me up for appearing out of uniform?"

———

Continue Reading *Ships Passing*, My Mira Book 4:
dustinstevens.com/SPam

Thank You

Aloha again!

If you're reading this, that likely means you read the first two install-ments of the *My Mira* saga and found it worthy of continuing. Thank you. I truly do appreciate it.

By now, I'm sure you know kind of what I'm going for with this story, and that you're finding it enjoyable. As I mentioned in the past, this was based off of really immersing myself in a Netflix saga this past winter, and wanting to put together something almost episodic nature. A form that was apart from other series I work on, where we get glimpses of a character and how they change over time, but only in spurts spread over a number of years.

With this particular work, I wanted to put together a full story, with a main character whose motivations and traits are fully fleshed, but also with a host of other storylines that contribute just as richly.

Hopefully, that is beginning to materialize here.

As I do each time (in a move I realize is a bit unorthodox), if you would be so kind, I would greatly appreciate any thoughts you might have on this. Reviews really do drive the entire indie publishing system, beginning with Amazon and filtering out onto other platforms.

Perhaps even more importantly, I find the insight and ideas contained there invaluable. As I always say, I might be one of the few that truly reads every review, a practice I promise to continue moving forward.

Until next time…happy trails,

Dustin

Free Book

Sign up for my newsletter and receive a FREE copy of my first bestseller – and still one of my personal favorites – *21 Hours:* dustinstevens.com/DS21Free

About the Author

Dustin Stevens is the author of more than 70 novels, the vast majority having become #1 Amazon bestsellers, including the Reed & Billie and Hawk Tate series. *The Boat Man*, the first release in the best-selling Reed & Billie series, was named an Indie Award winner for E-Book fiction. The freestanding work *The Debt* was named an Independent Author Network action/adventure novel of the year and *The Exchange* was recognized for independent E-Book fiction.

He also writes thrillers and assorted other stories under the pseudonym TR Kohler.

A member of the Mystery Writers of America and International Thriller Writers, he resides in Honolulu, Hawaii.

Let's Keep in Touch:
Website: dustinstevens.com
Facebook: dustinstevens.com/fcbk
Instagram: dustinstevens.com/DSinsta

Dustin's Books

Works Written by Dustin Stevens:

Reed & Billie Novels:

The Boat Man

The Good Son

The Kid

The Partnership

Justice

The Scorekeeper

The Bear

The Driver

The Promisor

The Ghost

The Family

The Cat

The Shadow

Hawk Tate Novels:

Cold Fire

Cover Fire

Fire and Ice

Hellfire

Home Fire

Wild Fire

Friendly Fire

Catching Fire

Forest Fire

Zoo Crew Novels:

The Zoo Crew

Dead Peasants

Tracer

The Glue Guy

Moonblink

The Shuffle

Swatted

Ham Novels:

HAM

EVEN

RULES

HOME

GONE

DEAL

My Mira Saga:

Spare Change

Office Visit

Fair Trade

Ships Passing

Warning Shot

Battle Cry

Steel Trap

Iron Men

Until Death

Night Novels:

Overlook

Decisions

Twelve

Hobby Lobby Mysteries:

The Exchange

Badger Games

Standalone Thrillers:

Moonshine Creek

The Subway

The Ring

Peeping Thoms

One Last Day

Shoot to Wound

The Debt

Going Viral

Liberation Day

Motive

21 Hours

Catastrophic

Four

Standalone Dramas:

Quarterback

Be My Eyes

Ohana

Just A Game

Scars and Stars

Children's Books w/ Maddie Stevens:

Danny the Daydreamer...Goes to the Grammy's

Danny the Daydreamer...Visits the Old West

Works Written by T.R. Kohler:

Hunter Series:

The Hunter

Street Divorce

Jumper Series:

Into The Jungle

Out To Sea

Bulletproof Series:

Mike's Place

Translator Series:

The Translator

The Confession

Made in the USA
Monee, IL
13 July 2025

21069008R00111